FATHERLESS

JOHN PASCAL

Defend the cause of the
Weak and fatherless. PS 82:3

For Dove –

John Pascal

1

FATHERLESS

August, 2017

First edition

ISBN# 13: 978-0692940303

Copyright pending

John Pascal Books
JOHNPASCAL.com

Bible quotations from "New International Version."
Copyright 1984, Zondervan Corp.

FLUSHED

The fire truck maneuvered through the cars, trucks and busy pedestrians in Manhattans' Upper East Side, lights flashing and emitting brief siren blips. Mike hit the horn at the next intersection. His fingers ruffled his curly red hair. "Darn cabs. They think they own this place."

Jim responded, "Easy, Mike. They know we're not heading for a fire. They got cabbie intuition."

Jim was tall and lean. He lowered dark eyebrows, and turned to his friend Ray beside him. "Getting back to your volunteer gig, my friend, don't tell me you're going into that neighborhood alone at night." He gestured with both hands. "Ray, why not just wait until your afternoon off?"

Mike issued a loud "WOONK!" as they approached an intersection. Tom, an athletic black man, tapped Mike on the shoulder. "Hey, do you *have* to? We're on the way home, already."

Mike heaved with laughter. "It's for the *kids*, Tom." He pointed at some waving children. "They all want to drive this thing one day." Another "WOONK."

"Oh yeah?" Tom chuckled. "See that tenement? In *this* neighborhood the kids all want to be pimps and gangsters when they grow up."

Jim was still focused on Ray. "Look, my gig's early in the morning, right near a subway stop where there are plenty of people around. No offense, but you look as tough as Woody Allen to these New Yorkers."

"Then they'd love me, right? Jim, ease up. I'm only supposed to give a care assist to this old lady. They have a helper for her weekdays. I'll only be checking on her one evening and once on the weekend to help out, so what's the problem? Anyway, what do you *married* men do after dinner?"

"Watch sitcoms mostly."

"Nothing like quality time." Ray adjusted his glasses and grinned. "I can do that and stay single."

"A bachelor wouldn't understand what it means to us." Jim waved at him with the back of his hand. "Once the little one's tucked in, Mary and I get to snuggle on the couch together, watch TV and talk about our day. I admit it's nothing a dead poet would write about, but it's our together time and a peaceful way to unwind. Besides, I really like the feel of her next to me."

Mike boomed the announcement. "Well, here we are: brave knights returning back home after saving the felines of the world." He swung the big truck into the garage bay. "I hope everyone remembers where we left our card game."

The four men poured out of their vehicle and pounded up the fire station stairs, Mike in the lead.

"Don't let Mike get there first," Tom hollered. "He'll check our cards."

Mike yelled back. "Will not. What do you take me for?"

"Someone who wins too much." The others laughed.

Ray surveyed the poker game laid out on the kitchen table. "Relax, it's just like we left it." He scratched through his yellow hair. "But, Tom's cards look a bit scattered."

Tom swung a chair over with a muscled forearm, pulled off his fire jacket and placed it on the chair back. He scowled at the table. "Nah, I just got up too quick when we got the call." He headed for the refrigerator. "Fresh round of cokes for everyone?"

Ray raised a finger. "Uh…"

"Yeah, I know, I know. Orange soda. We all know you're weird, Ray. And you didn't even have to come with us this time."

Ray slid into his chair and took a quick look at his cards. "Why? Just because it was only a cat in a tree? You don't understand. As a paramedic I had to give *psychological* therapy to the little girl, and Jim could have ended up with cat scratches. Besides, *none* of you would believe I wouldn't peek at the cards when you were gone, right?"

Mike chuckled. "Got that right."

Tom returned to the table with the sodas and a bag of Fritos under his elbow. He dropped the chips in the center, but delicately delivered the orange soda to Ray with a grin. "And *this* is for our psychiatrist."

Mike's twinkling blue eyes squinted from his ruddy face while he examined his cards close to his chest. "Might as well finish this up, guys." He pulled the bag open and crunched on a chip. "You're due for a draw, Jim."

Jim drew a card, thought for a moment, and casually moved two Hershey Kisses to the center. "I'll bet ten million."

Mike shook his head. "The kisses are only *one* million. Granola bars are five, remember?"

"Oh, right, and you won most of those already. Two million it is then."

Mike moved two kisses and five M&Ms toward the pile. "I got your two and I raise you five hundred thousand."

Tom shrugged and put his cards down. "I'm out."

Ray studied his cards. "All I have is my last granola bar." He took a swig of orange soda and slid the bar to the center. "Okay, I'll double your bet, Mike."

Mike coughed and studied Ray for a thoughtful moment. He pushed two more Kisses and five M&Ms into the pot pile. He raised his eyebrows at Jim who was folding his cards with a sigh. "Out," said Jim.

Mike tilted his head toward Ray and grinned. "Looks like I'm calling our psychiatrist." He drawled, "Whacha got, podner?"

With a sheepish smile Ray laid down a pair of aces. Mike nodded and glanced at the other two. "Now, say what you will about Ray. Our psychic healer does bluff well."

Mike laid out a full flush and swept the sugary pile toward himself with a laugh. "Oh, lookie, now I'm ready for Halloween."

Tom collected the cards. "So, we're flushed. You'd think he'd let one of us win sometime just to be nice. Giants kickoff in five, guys." He grabbed his drink, went into the lounge and plopped onto the sofa.

Mike began sweeping his loot into a bag and glanced at Jim. "So, is it true you two religious nuts are heading out into our fair city to save the world?"

Jim laughed. "Religious nuts? You mean because Ray and I go to church on Sundays?"

"Yeah, but you guys are really serious about it. I go to mass every week, but *your* church's sending you two out like apostles, right?"

"Well, not quite. Our Christian Fellowship is encouraging us to get out there and bear fruit in the kingdom, you know, do something good for humanity beyond our comfort zone."

Mike went to his locker along one wall and dropped his bag inside. "Comfort zone? What exactly is that, Jim?"

"I'll be helping out in the food service line at a homeless shelter. I plan to overcome my shyness and tell someone about Jesus while I'm there."

Ray took some chips out of their common bag and passed them on before he joined Tom on the couch with Mike right behind him. "Pastor suggested I call on hospice patients because I'm a paramedic, Mike. I'll be up above the park checking in on this elderly lady tomorrow night."

Mike scowled. "Sounds really boring. At North General Hospital?"

"No, they're home visits. She lives in a condo in Harlem."

"What?!" Mike swiveled toward Ray. "You're not thinking of driving there alone at night, are you?"

"Not real late, and it's not far from Fifth Avenue, a few blocks north of the park. We've been near there on fire calls before, and I'm going around eight. Besides, I expect her condo has a parking garage."

Mike rolled his eyes at the ceiling. "Really? You're expecting some upscale condominium in that part of the city? Here, give me the address."

Ray wrote it on a scrap of paper and handed it to Mike who studied at it with furrowed brows. "Did anyone ever look at the map of street gangs I put inside the bathroom door?" Silence. "Okay, I'm going to pee and check this out."

Mike returned and had Jim mute the TV amid groans of protest. "A quick lesson from my brother, the cop. Some white guy parks in the middle of gang territory at night and they'll probably leave him alone. They figure he's either a customer or a cop."

Ray said, "Good, that's settled. Look, they're about to kick off."

"Ray, where you don't want to be is *in between* gang territories. The disputed areas are where they love to shoot at each other, and that's where you're going."

"Oh, stop worrying. They can see I'm no gang member."

"And you're not going to listen to *any* advice we give, are you? Here, gimme the remote."

Tom looked at Ray and crossed his eyes.

Jim said, "Mike, I tried to tell him. You know the city better than anyone and you think it's really dangerous, don't you? What would be your advice?"

Mike leveled a steady gaze at Ray, loudly crunching a Frito chip for emphasis. "My advice? I'd say, first we all *pray*, and second, we put an ad in tomorrow's paper for our next paramedic." He clicked the sound back on.

COMFORT ZONE

Ray's car zigzagged through Harlem's dimly lit streets, his Garmin navigator periodically announcing loss of signal. He noticed homeless men arranging their spots to spend the night at alleyway entrances while shops clanged their steel protective gates shut.

While stopped at a traffic light, a gang of bandana-wearing teens began to cross in front of him but surrounded his car and leered in. Briefly, they rapped on his hood with something metal, beating out a rhythm and dancing away to the beat. Some spun around to glare back, deliver departing curse words, hand signs and laughter.

So, this is the "good" part of town, right in the center of their territory like Mike said. These guys never bothered us in the paramedic van. At the next light he had to wait even after it changed. An old woman slowly crossed in front of him, limping behind a grocery cart brim full of all her worldly goods.

Pastor Will had a funny expression when he said: "If you really want to do the Lord's work, step out of your comfort zone." Okay, Lord. Here I am.

Finally, he turned away from the shops. Brownstone tenements were on both sides, and shortly, his electronic navigator announced: "You have arrived at your destination."

He glanced around. *Gates of Hell, perhaps?* Ray pulled into a space hoping he was far enough from the hydrant. *Could get a ticket here, but come to think of it, maybe I wish there were police around.*

Ray compared the street number to his notes and looked around for pedestrians. Nobody. He surveyed the old building noting one window was boarded up. *This is a condominium? I hope they'll at least have security.*

Quickly, he grabbed his paramedic bag, chirped on the car alarm and hastened up the steps to the front entrance. The old oak door was unlocked and he entered an empty lobby. Weathered paint peeling off decorations remaining from the Art Deco era defined the state of the building. Stale, musty air twinged his nostrils and wooden floorboards creaked under every step. *Guess I can forget security, huh?* He smirked.

Ray leaned on the dust-streaked reception desk. He could see light coming through an open door behind the counter. Leaning forward, a man in uniform came into view. He sat at a table munching a slice of pizza. The man looked up at him and tossed his head. "Yeah?"

"Ray Johnson from the Hospice Volunteers, calling on a Mrs. Garcia in 304." He held up an ID certificate.

The guard chewed, swallowed and seemed to digest the information. He didn't get up to look at the document but waved the back of his hand at him. "Sure, sure. Elevator's down the hall."

Ray took his bag and found he was following a couple who had come in after him. Together they stood listening to the elevator's ominous grinding noise. The girl appeared to be a teenager. She had a long face and straight hair, mostly dyed red. A wig, he thought. She sported tight black shorts, high heels and eye-watering perfume.

He coughed. "Hope this elevator works." They ignored him.

Ray tried to make eye contact, but she continued to stare at the floor with an ugly frown. Water or tears caused streaks in her makeup revealing freckles on the side of her nose. The man, maybe late fifties, was smiling and rubbing her shoulder.

She got on the elevator first, punched a button and said without looking up, "What floor?"

"Three, thanks."

She nodded, stepped back and stood motionless while the old lift ground its way upward and bounced to a stop on the third floor. As the door opened, the girl turned to go out and shot him a glance. Her eye contact came and went in half a second but Ray was frozen by her fleeting expression. It said: "*Help.*"

HOSPICE

Ray checked the wall sign for apartment numbers, looked down the hall and saw the girl opening a door with a key. Her head continued to hang down even as she entered with the man who gave her a shove, laughed and stepped in.

When he found 304, he realized he was right next door to the apartment where the couple had entered. Noting the nameplates under each doorbell, his said "Garcia," hers had a photo of lips. His ring was answered by a distant "Just a minute."

Shortly, he heard a closer, "Who is it?"

"Mister Johnson from Hospice."

After a few grunts near the peephole, bolts were sliding and chains were clinking. The door cracked open and an old woman's voice said, "Okay, come on in."

Mrs. Garcia greeted him from her wheelchair sporting a ball of curly white hair and a yellow-toothed smile. "Well, you're a handsome one. Call me Winnie. Slide the deadbolt if you will."

Her motorized chair swiveled around and headed for the living room. He replied to her back. "I'm Ray. Nice to meet you."

"What's in the big bag?"

"My paramedic tools. Thought it might come in handy."

"Maybe, maybe not." She turned her chair to face a couch, gestured for him to sit and pouted her lips. "Don't think I need nothing, so, why exactly did they send you here?"

Ray had to smile at her brashness. "I'm really not sure, Winnie. This is my first time as a volunteer, but they said I was supposed to keep you company for a couple of hours and help out where I can. They mentioned reading and cooking."

"So, you don't know *nothing*, huh. Oh, I get it," Winnie chuckled. She looked up at the ceiling dropped her jaw and clasped her hands together. "You're here so the poor old broad won't kick off all alone with no one to care." She sang the "all alone" part.

His turn to laugh. "Not exactly the way the association phrased it. They said you wanted to stay in your home as long as you could, and we hope can help you with that."

"Okay, now you're making sense. If no one boots me out because you're here, I'll be on my best behavior."

"Who would want to evict you?"

"My 'la-te-da' son in Brooklyn Heights for one. 'Ma needs to be in a nursing home.' He sells that crap to anyone who'll listen."

"Well, in all fairness, your strength might fail later, Mrs. Garcia. You've got cancer, right?"

"Call me Winnie or next time I'll clonk you with that cane. Yeah, end stage colon cancer, they said. Shameless, crazy intestine cells forgot about the job God gave 'em. Now they're having a party in my long bones digesting them. My doctor's afraid I'll break my leg if I walk too much."

"Yes, I'm sure he's concerned about the possibility, especially when you're alone."

"Well, I told him not to worry." She jiggled a call button hanging from a necklace. "I just press this little dingle and all you good looking hunks come running in to save me."

Winnie gave him a big grin, got up with a slight wince and leaned on her cane. "Anyway, I can walk. Can I get you some coffee?"

"I think that's my job while I'm here. Are you in much pain?"

"Nothing three Advils can't handle." She waved her cane toward the next room. "On second thought, just so you don't feel completely useless, why don't you get us a couple of beers from the fridge, huh?"

When Ray came back with the bottles, she was sitting on the couch, patting the cushion next to her. He handed her a beer with a grin. "I'm guessing you drink from the bottle."

Winnie smirked. After he sat down, she clinked bottles with him. "Right on. I like you already so I won't tell Hospice you drink on the job. But, tell me all about yourself. I gather you're single."

"Only if you promise to do the same. And how do you know I'm not married?"

She chuckled. "Eighty six years of experience. You look kinda bookish. You're cute but naive. Spill me the bio, huh?"

"I'm thirty two and raised in West Virginia. I love science and majored in it at college. I did a stint in the army as a corpsman and checked for a job when I got out three years ago. That landed me here."

"And your love life?"

Ray shook his head, smiling. "I dated a nurse at Metropolitan Hospital for about a year, but she left me for a doctor a few months ago, and I can't believe I'm telling you this."

"No, see, *now* we're having fun. You're supposed to cheer me up and it's working, but I'm real sorry the girl left you."

"No problem, but you promised to tell me about *your* intimate details next, say why you ended up here, for instance. But before you start, do you know who lives in the apartment next to you?" He gestured with his thumb.

"No one. Some syndicate owns it."

"Looked like a father and daughter walked in there when I came."

Winnie shrieked with laughter and slapped her knee. "Oh man, you really are the West Virginia hick. Never saw a hooker before? Maybe you need new glasses."

"Well I…I kinda thought that was probably it, but I don't like to judge."

Her expression softened into a motherly smile. "Yeah, well, you're a real sweet kid. Didn't mean to offend."

Winnie took a swig of beer. "So, that apartment is one they use to drop off their 'working girls'. It's hard to believe, but when this building was put up in the twenties it was a nice place to live. My father bought this unit when it went condo in the sixties, but the walls are paper thin."

"That must be annoying."

"Ya think? I can hear them at night so I'm glad my bedroom's on the other side. Of course *there* I hear a couple shouting at each other in Spanish."

Ray gave a slow shrug and put his beer down on the coffee table. "Look, I'm supposed to help with your medical care too. You have a colostomy bag, right?"

"Yep, and it's a real pain, too." Winnie pulled up her shirt to show him. "Been itching lately."

Ray opened his bag, put it next to her and knelt on the floor to face her. "I can see why. There's a little infection going on under the tape."

He quickly removed the dressing, applied antiseptic around the portal and redressed the site. "This paper tape will itch less but it doesn't stay on as well so I'll give you the roll to patch it if you need to."

"Hey, you're good. How often are you coming around?"

"Wednesday nights and Saturday noon, but Winnie, don't pretend you don't remember promising to tell me about yourself."

She chuckled. "Like anyone's really interested." That was met by a silent, expectant stare. "Okay, well, I've lived here like forever. My husband, Matt, died two years ago and now I'm fixin' to join him. That's about it."

Ray shook his head. "That's only the last chapter."

"Oh, all right. I was a school principal before I retired, and I almost got fired for mentioning Jesus once. Just once. Can you believe it? I have only one son who's a vice president at a bank. He's rejected God and never learned any manners.

"There's two grandchildren, though. Fortunately *their* mother did a better job than I did. Stanley's in the Air Force. He's stationed at Nellis Air Base and got married last year. I'm hoping for some great grandkids but I probably won't live to give them a cuddle."

"So, I guess you don't get to see much of your Airman, huh?"

"Yeah, and I miss seeing his square jaw and crew cut, but my granddaughter, Sophie, lives nearby. She's twenty eight, a church-goer and a real sweetheart."

"Oh, right. Hospice said you had a daughter who helps."

"She sure does. Sophie comes by twice a week for lunch and sometimes weekends too. She works for a title company and insists she'll stay a career woman, but I know she'd also like to be a wife and mother. That girl's real fussy, but she just needs to meet the right gentleman." Winnie grinned at Ray. "You know, someone like a good hearted paramedic."

Ray laughed.

GRILLIN'

Two weeks had passed and the fire crew sat at their table eating the sandwiches Tom prepared. Speaking with his mouth full, Jim turned to Ray and mumbled. "Brought a homeless man to Jesus yesterday."

"No kidding," Ray responded. "I think you picked the better mission. My old lady's already a Christian, and she's a real trip."

Tom came in from the kitchen with three Cokes and an orange soda. He slid into his chair and spoke as he passed out the drinks. "So, Ray, despite Mike's dire prediction, here you are, alive and well."

"Yeah, so far the worst thing was getting my car keyed, but last Saturday I met a few of the roving teens, two black boys. They seemed surprised that an adult would be even talking to them, much less a white guy. I was kinda surprised at myself, too. Anyway, I shot a few hoops with the boys and said maybe I'll show them the fire station one day. Can't believe I said that but at least, I think they'll leave my car alone."

Rapid toenail clicks resounded up their stairs. Jim raised a finger. "Oops, Mack got out of the Chief's office again. Must have pushed around the barricade."

The yellow lab came over to them, vigorously wagging his tail. Tom chuckled. "He can smell cold cuts a block away."

Jim gave Mack a little rough scratching on his shoulder blades and slipped him half a slice of turkey breast. "Look, Ray, keep up your friendship with the boys. Maybe you'll get a chance to talk to someone about God after all."

"I doubt it, but…" He squinted at Mike. "You've been uncommonly quiet today."

Mike shrugged. "Hey, I'm just glad you're still alive." He looked up at the ceiling and blew out through his cheeks.

Ray sighed. "*What,* Mike?"

Mike gave his hand a little toss in the air. "Don't want to say nothing discouraging to you hardworking apostles."

"Oh, go ahead." Ray chuckled. "Why be shy for the first time in your life?"

Mike scowled. "Look, I think it's great you two going out and helping people, I do, but you're wasting your time telling them about God and all."

Jim chimed in, "Really, Mike. I'd really like to know why you think so."

"Ah, 'cause they all say they love Jesus just to make you happy and get a bigger handout."

Jim shook his head. "Not so with the homeless, well most of them. Some really are believers already, and if anyone is faking it, I'd spot em' as easy as spotting you dancing in the Radio City chorus line."

"All right, maybe you *can* get to some of the homeless, but Ray should stay away from those gangs." He pointed a finger at Ray. "I heard the Puerto Rican ones are even more dangerous than the blacks."

"Really." Ray took a swig of orange soda. "Well, someone forgot to tell these boys. I've seen them playing together with whites and even an Asian—just friends from school, I think. I know they get into mischief, but I haven't heard any hints of real crime. Of course, as you say, I'm in the border between territories."

"Ray," Mike shook his head. "Ray, these are *not* prep school kids. You're not so naive you don't know they smoke pot and grab old ladies purses."

"Sonny, I think he's their leader, did ask what was in my bag."

"And yer lucky you still have it."

Ray shook his head. "Ah, you're so *negative*. I showed them what a paramedic carries. They just wanted to know more about what I do, but..." He grimaced at Mike. "Okay, I'll admit it. Sonny did smell of pot."

Mike lifted his hands. His grin said, "I told you so."

SATURDAY

Ray smiled at the abundance of parking spaces he found on the weekend. He pulled into one near the condo where two familiar black youths were playing basketball in an alley with a makeshift net. As he lifted his paramedic bag from the back seat, the taller boy came over bouncing his ball. It was Sonny.

"Uh, Mister Johnson," he said. He avoided eye contact and kept dribbling. "Can I ask you something?"

"Sure, shoot."

"Did you say you could show me and my brother your firehouse?" He bounce-passed the ball to Ray and displayed a white toothy grin.

Ray harrumphed and dribbled a few times on the side walk. "I'll have to ask the Chief, but if it's okay, sure, I'll show you around." He glanced at the younger boy who had come over. "This your brother?"

"Clyde? Yeah, he's fourteen"

Clyde was silently studying the rooftops. Ray shot the ball to him and cried, "Heads up, Clyde."

He just missed catching it and had to chase the ball down the sidewalk. Ray and Sonny laughed. "Look, I have to make lunch for Winnie right now, but I'll call my Chief. I'll be back here around two thirty and let you know."

Ray was feeling strangely euphoric when he gave the "Knickerbocker Beer nock" on her door, but was surprised and speechless for a moment. This time he was greeted by the sparkling dark eyes and smile of a young woman.

"Ah, you must be Ray." She held out her hand to shake his. "I'm Sophie. Grandma told me all about you."

"Uh, hi."

She swirled around with a swish of long black hair. "Come on in. You're just in time for lunch."

Winnie displayed a silly grin from her wheelchair as Ray approached. He squinted at her, replying to Sophie, "You know you can't believe anything your grandmother says, don't you?"

Sophie tittered and headed for the kitchen. "I'm almost ready. I'll call you to help serve in a minute."

Ray kept his squint firmly pointed at Winnie. "You said Sophie makes supper. I'm supposed to do lunch. Do I detect mischief in those eyes?"

Winnie shrugged with a "who knows?" pout. "Sometimes she likes more time with her grandmom, Ray. Sophie's going shopping for me after lunch. Maybe you could help her with that."

"Oh, you're *so* transparent." He chuckled. "Sorry, but I have to take some boys I met on the street to the firehouse this afternoon, so your plans are foiled. Let me see your dressing."

He knelt and added strips of tape to replace those peeling off. "There. No infection in sight, so you're good until the nurse comes next week." He wheeled her to the bathroom. "Let's wash up for lunch."

When she finished, Winnie asked to be walked to the table, so Ray took one hand and put his arm around her waist. "Something smells good in the kitchen," he said.

As he sat her down at the table, she rolled up some "big eyes" toward him. "Sophie's been to cooking school." Ray's head shook as he chuckled.

A call from the kitchen summoned him. Sophie's back was turned and she was stirring a pot. She wore a conservative blue-gray dress protected by an apron. He peered into the pot and asked, "What is that heavenly aroma?"

"The sauce for Chicken Marsala." She pointed to three plates with chicken breasts on a bed of noodles. "Could you take those in and come back to toss the salad?"

When Ray was tossing the salad, he said, "This sure is a fancier lunch than I would have made."

"You probably noticed Granny's appetite is waning." She poured the sauce into a gravy boat. "I just want her to enjoy some meals while she can."

"Well, I'm glad to enjoy them with her."

Sophie pointed to a glass pitcher. "Bring in the iced tea. Oh, and as you can see, Granny is trying to fix me up again. I know she's terminal, but please, just ignore her."

Their eyes met. "Well sure, unless of course, it's her dying wish." He gave Sophie his best grin. She returned a suppressed chuckle-snort.

FIREHOUSE

Sonny and Clyde were waiting on the steps for Ray to come out of Winnie's condo.

Clyde looked up at his brother, his eyes wide. "Think he'll let us come?"

Sonny was watching a woman walking across the street. "Ah, who knows? I'm only going 'cause I don't meet the Creeds family boss until tomorrow. Heard they romanced two more girls for the Big Guy. Skeeze was hinting I might get to, you know, play with one of them."

"Geeze, really? Sounds like you're in already. What will ya hafta do for initiation?"

"It ain't easy, bro. Maybe rob a store, lasso a runaway or even beat up a Blade. Gonna be something showy, anyway."

Clyde stared at his brother in silent admiration, but just then, Ray came out and stood on the porch. Sonny leaned against the railing real casual, adjusted his green headband and grunted: "Chief say it's okay?"

"We're good for an hour. Let's go."

Clyde dropped his jaw. "Yeah, but…"

Sonny broke in. "But you gotta check in with *our* chief first."

Ray looked puzzled. "You have a Chief?"

The boys' eyes dropped. Clyde scuffed a shoe. "I know we shouldn't hafta, but…"

Sonny coughed and made eye contact. "We hafta run you by our grandma first. No problem, but she'd spaz out if we just left."

"Oh, I get it. You didn't ask her yet?"

"Sure we did."

"And she said?"

"You ain't gettin' in no strange white man's car less I check him out first."

Ray laughed. "All right then. Let's go and get me checked. How far away?"

Clyde's face brightened. "Really? You'll *come*?" They sped down the steps ahead of him. "Just a couple of blocks. Short walk."

They led him to a tall tenement building. Two young girls were playing Hop Scotch on the sidewalk outside. "Short one's my sister," Clyde offered.

At the top of the entrance stairs Sonny pulled off his headband, folded it neatly and carefully slid it in his pocket. Ray asked, "Is that special?"

Clyde blurted out; "Oh yeah. It's a *Creed* marker. They might take Sonny in if..."

He stopped with a swat on the arm from his brother. "Shut up! You want Grandma to hear?"

"Sorry." Clyde looked up at Ray. "He's not even sixteen yet, but they might take him early."

Another swat. "Shut up, I said. Come on. We're going in."

The grandmother was slight of build and well wrinkled. She wore an African print dress and a pink headband to hold back her Afro. With wheezing breaths, she silently looked Ray up and down. He ventured to extend his hand. "Hello, I'm Raymond Johnson."

"I'm Grandma Helen." She didn't take the hand but motioned for him to come in. "You like some tea?"

"I'd love some, Helen."

She pointed a finger at Sonny. "Pot's on the stove. Bring it in on the tray. You two can have some Pepsis. No sweets."

Her apartment was truly Spartan. Her only decorations were some African masks and a large photo of a boy in a frame with fake flowers around it, her son, he figured.

The inquisition would begin in the living room across a coffee table. Helen sighed and scowled at Ray. "As you can see, I got three kids to tend. Long story, but I just want to keep em alive 'till they're eighteen. I'm not well and who knows if I'll make it.

So why are you in this neighborhood and what you want with my boys?"

"I come here as a hospice volunteer for a Mrs. Garcia a few blocks away. I'm here on Sat…"

"*Winifred* Garcia?"

"You know her?"

"Sure. She was the principal at my son's high school when he was alive. God rest his soul. She really stirred that place up.

"I'll allow she's opinionated, but she's got a good heart in there. Garcia was a Puerto Rican principal at a mostly black school. Some hated her, some loved her."

Sonny had placed the tray on the coffee table and knew to pour two cups. He looked at his grandmother. "Can we go to my room?"

"Sit. Listen."

Ray said, "So how did you get along with Winnie?"

Helen snorted at her name in the familiar. "Winnie, huh? We sure never called her that, but I say, looking back, she did a good job. She fired one of the black teachers, though. Sure made a lot of people mad. Looking back, she was right, I guess."

"Doesn't sound like she had an easy job."

Helen chuckled. "No. What did you say about a hospital?"

Ray sipped some tea. "Hospice. It's a service for those who are dying."

Helen sighed, put down her cup and leaned back. "Sorry to hear that. Maybe I should pay her a visit. What do you think?"

Ray made his voice sound serious. "I'm sure Mrs. Garcia would like that."

Helen smiled. "So it's *Winnie* now, is it?" She leaned forward and grasped both knees. "You really taking my boys to the firehouse?"

"Right now if it's okay with you."

Helen fixed her gaze on the boys and scowled. "Okay then. Maybe they'll learn something useful, but be back in a couple of hours, all right?"

The boys scurried to her side and gave her a quick hug. "Thanks, Grandma," they said together.

Sonny and Clyde murmured oohs and ahs as they walked into the firehouse and gaped at the trucks and equipment. Ray took them to the Chief's office first for an official welcome. "Hi, boys. Glad to have you visit. You're welcome anytime even if you're friends of Ray, here."

Clyde and Sonny were on their knees getting sloppy kisses from his dog, but Sonny ventured, "Yes, Sir. Real cool stuff you got here."

Ray showed them his paramedic van and his rescue equipment, but the trucks next to it dwarfed the van. The kids were fascinated by the big, the red and the shiny. Ray told them all about the firemen's jobs, but most of the questions were about the big, the red and the shiny.

Just as he was about to usher them out, the Holy Spirit gave Ray one of those "nudges," a big one. It smacked him to one side, turned him around and headed him toward the big hook and ladder truck where Tom Scott was working. Tom was a handsome, black man vigorously polishing one of the chrome side tanks.

Ray turned to the boys, enthusiasm in his voice. "Hey, I saved the best for last guys. Mister Scott here steers the back of this monster sitting way up on top and out in the open."

As they approached, Tom put his rag aside and grinned. "Well, I'll be. You two look just like my boys. I'm Tom. How's the tour going?

Sonny looked up at him, awe and admiration coming over his face. "Just fine, Mister Scott."

Clyde pointed up. "You really ride up *there*?"

Tom peered into his excited eyes. "Absolutely, and I'll take you up—unless you're afraid, of course."

"No, no. Up *there,* really?"

Tom put his hands on their shoulders and guided them to the back of the truck. He flashed a wink back at Ray. "See this ladder? What's your name?"

"Clyde."

"Okay, Clyde. You go up first and stand on the runway you'll see. We'll be right behind you."

Clyde flew up the narrow ladder on the back of the truck, and raised his arms in triumph when he reached the top.

Tom chuckled. "Don't put your hands on anything that shines like a mirror, or you'll spend the afternoon polishing, okay?"

Clyde started to walk down the gangway but Tom called out, "Easy, man. We'll be right there."

Sonny did his best to look unimpressed, but joy was all over his face when he sat on the wheel seat. "Any chance we could hit the horn?"

Tom shook his head. "Not inside here. We'd be deaf for a week."

When the boys finally came down, Tom put his hands on each shoulder and looked from one to the other. "Hey, you guys, two weeks from Sunday we're having our annual barbeque at Carl Schurz Park by the river."

Tom looked at Ray. "You think you could have these two troublemakers there by three? Maybe they could ride back with us in the tanker."

"But, you're going with your family, aren't you?"

"Mona will drive our guys over." He glanced at the boys giving them a serious look. "I could use help with the siren if you're coming."

The boys bestowed an open-mouthed look of adoration on Tom, nodding their heads, "yes." Today, at least, Ray knew he had done something right.

KITTEN

Ray arrived at Winnie's a little late Wednesday evening and found her outside on the front porch, sitting in her wheelchair waving hello. "Sorry, I'm late. I'll read you an extra chapter if you want. What are you doing out here?"

"It's cool and breezy tonight. I just like to sit and listen to the music."

"Music? All I hear is kids playing in the alley."

"Yes."

Ray searched for meaning, then smiled. "I could get a chair and sit with you out here if you like."

Winnie rolled her eyes up at him. "You're sweet. No, let's go in and make some coffee."

When they got to her apartment, Ray shook his head at the shouts coming through the walls. "Sounds like I'll have to yell to read your story. That's some argument they're having next door."

"Yeah, usually it's the married couple on the other side, but I have an idea how you can help."

"Sure. Oh, wait, it sounds like they're quiet again. What's the plan?"

She reached the couch, turned to face him and set the brake on her chair. Pointing a finger, she said, "There's an oriental rug in that hall closet. If you take that picture off the wall and nail up the rug, it should help to muffle the sounds. Hammer and nails in the bottom kitchen drawer."

"Sounds easy enough. How are you feeling today?"

"Eeech, passable. I get short-winded and tired when I walk. Doctor said my lungs are involved with the cancer now, so it's no surprise. But, say, thanks for sending Helen Jackson to visit me. Her son was tragically smart and immoral. When he died of a drug, it overdose was no surprise to me. Anyway, we had a nice chat about old times."

"Sorry to hear your cancer is spreading like that. We'll do some extra prayer time, but listen, I'm impressed by your great attitude going through all this, Winnie."

She chuckled. "Dying is like sledding down a rough hill. You know the crash at the bottom is coming, but you still try and avoid the boulders. Tell me. How are things going with *you,* young man?"

"Same eeech for me. Somehow I got tangled up with Helen's grandkids kids I met on the street outside, but at least they keep an eye on my car when I'm in here. By the way, I asked Sophie out, but she turned me down."

Winnie laughed. "She did, huh. Ray, did you ever play the ring toss at Coney Island?"

"No, but a couple of times at a county fair."

"Win a prize?"

"I did. What of it?"

Winnie had a bout of coughing and Ray got her a tissue. "But, Ray, did you win on your *first* try?"

"I see your point, but I don't think she's interested. I thanked her for the lunch she made me and told her I should take her to dinner in exchange."

"In *exchange?*" She coughed a little more and shook her head. "Oh, man, I'm sorry but that was lame, Ray."

"I thought I was being polite."

"Polite is how married couples act when they've been invited to a friends house. Pay attention. First, Sophie didn't make the lunch for *you*. No payback needed. Second, what happened to 'I'd like to get to know you. Will you have dinner with me Saturday?'"

"I admit, that *does* sound a lot smoother." He got up and hastened down the hall. "I'll get the rug out."

Ray was dragging the oriental out of the closet but dropped it at the sound of a loud scream from next door. A man shouted obscenities so loud it seemed there was no wall between them.

Suddenly, another scream. The wall shuddered from a huge crash, then a thump. Silence. "Winnie, I should call the cops. Wait, you call them. I better go see."

"Just a quick peek. Be careful. Want to take a gun?"

Ray flashed Winnie a look of disbelief at that remark but he cautiously opened the door. A large man was getting on the elevator down the hall. The door next to theirs was closed and locked. He knocked. No answer so he came back.

Winnie pointed. "Ray, take that green key on the peg by the door. It's a master. Should get you in."

"You have a..." Dismissing the question he spun around back to the neighbors door, opened it and found himself inside an almost dark room. What little light there was came from a Japanese lantern on the far wall swinging on a cord.

Ray found the ceiling light switch, flipped it on and gasped. She lay unconscious on the floor wearing only bra and panties and a sleeve tattoo on one arm, wrist to shoulder. He checked to see if she was breathing, carefully supported her neck and head, lifted her up and carried her around to Winnies'. He gently set her down on the couch.

Winnie was on her feet and announced, "I didn't call the police; I called Sophie." She had a throw blanket in her arms and covered the girl. "She's not dead, is she?"

"No, thank God, but I think the man I saw threw her against the wall. There's a huge dent in the drywall." Ray took

44

out a flashlight, held it to her face and raised each painted blue eyelid. "Pupils both equal and reactive to light. Normal respirations. Hopefully there's no concussion."

The blue lids began to flutter. "This girl's the one I saw on the elevator some nights back, Winnie. She's coming around."

Winnie had her phone in hand and sat back down on her wheelchair, coughing. Ray said, "Don't bother calling an ambulance. It's only a few blocks. I'll take her to the hospital myself as soon as I feel she's stable."

"Okay, but Sophie will be here in a minute. She can help."

The girl's perfectly coiffed, short hair was a shade of pink and had survived the trauma undisturbed. Ray wiped away the smeared lipstick and tended to a cut lip. "This girl bought a two hundred dollar hairdo but spent nothing on dental work, Winnie."

As he put on antiseptic and fixed a dressing on her forehead abrasion, the girl convulsed, coughed and moaned. Winnie said, "Oh, good, she's waking up. Can I get anything?"

"A bowl or small trash can in case she throws up."

Eyes still closed, the girl began to stir, mumbling, "You *knew* I don't do that one. You knew." Her body gave one general twitch, her eyes opened and she started to sit up. She emitted a moan and lay back against the pillow, her gaze fixed on Ray. "You my next John? I'm gonna need some time, fella."

"No, I'm Ray Johnson, a paramedic. You were knocked unconscious. What's your name?"

She started to put her left hand on her forehead but gave a short cry. "My wrist. Is it broken?"

Ray looked at the swollen, pink wrist. "Can't tell without an Xray. I'll wrap it for now. This woman is Winnie. We're in her apartment next door. What do we call you?"

"Kitten, Kitten Comfort. I remember, now. That 'f__g' bastard threw me against the wall." She opened up her right hand exposing a five dollar bill. "When I wouldn't do what he wanted he gave me this. That 's__t' head said it's all I was *worth*."

Winnie wheeled close to the girl and she placed a hand on her shoulder. "Oh, my dear, always remember: to Jesus you are priceless."

At this, Kitten sat up blinking her half inch eyelashes. "Whew, a little dizzy. Well, thanks for everything but I gotta get back."

Ray shook his head. "Not the best plan right now, Miss."

"It's the *only* plan, John. I gotta call—oh Jees, I remember. He smashed my phone. Can I use yours?"

Ray made sure he had close eye contact. "The only plan, Miss Kitten, is the hospital. You were unconscious and you might have a concussion and a broken arm."

"Yeah, well that's *nothing* compared to what a certain someone will do to me if I don't call in." The girl lunged up to her feet and began to stagger to the door with Ray right behind her.

"Gotta get my clothes and backpack," she mumbled.

There was a knock on the apartment door and it opened before she got there. Kitten fainted into Sophie's arms as she entered.

Ray and Sophie carried the girl back to the couch. Sophie gingerly put her head on the pillow and turned to her grandmother. "I'll get my overnight pajamas for her." She scowled at Ray. "You should have *told* me you already had a girlfriend."

He chuckled. "And Winnie should have told me about your sense of humor."

STATION BREAK

"So this homeless man is telling me how great his life is…" Jim gestured with his hands. "I mean, he's *homeless,* right? He rattles on all about how he likes having no responsibilities, and living on food stamps in complete freedom. Meanwhile, I'm wondering if he's just pulling my leg. Pass the doughnuts."

Mike slid the box toward him. "Well, maybe he has a point."

Tom shook his head. "Oh, come on. You know he's putting you on."

Jim pointed at Ray and spoke through his doughnut. "You might be right, but what does my 'out-of-our-comfort-zone' partner think?"

"He's dodging. He's really saying he's not buying what you're selling."

Jim smiled. "Exactly. The word is out about me evangelizing, and he doesn't want to hear it."

Tom said, "So you gave up?"

"Nope. I'll get my witness in later. Meanwhile, I let him ramble on about his happiness. The guy loves having an audience and waxes philosophical. Turns out he had two years of college and was in business before his finances collapsed and he turned to booze."

Ray slid the doughnuts past him. "None for me. Well, being a good listener is a ministry of sorts, Jim. You'll get to talk about God some other time."

"Oh, I will." Jim squinted at Ray. "You look tired, man. How's it going with your hospice lady?"

"With her? Fine. She knows more about Jesus than I do." Ray sighed. "My problem yesterday was stumbling over a prostitute."

Laughter broke out and Ray waved his hands at them. "Wait, what I mean is, last night this girl got beat up in the apartment next door, and I had to take her to the hospital. Her life is a *real* mess. Worse than your philosopher."

Mike cocked his head and asked, "And that's the end of your story, right?" Ray sat in silence. Mike persisted. "Right?"

Ray looked up at the ceiling. "Maybe it should be, but I'm feeling called to do something more to help her. She's just a teenager, a *young* teenager."

Mike's hand came down on the table and he shook his head. "No, Ray, you can't help those hookers. I tried once myself. It's like talking to zombies. Forget about it."

Jim raised a finger. "No one is beyond help, Mike. Maybe God *does* want Ray to try and help the kid."

Ray tossed his hands in the air. "Well, look guys, I have no idea what I'm going to do, but I think I'll visit her at the hospital after my shift. Talking can't hurt. Maybe she'll consider changing her life after almost being killed. We'll see what hap..."

Their Alert Bell went off and Mike hastened to the red phone on the wall. "Paramedic call. There's been a street shooting. Meet Bill in the van. Sounds like it's near your hospice lady, Ray."

REALITY

Ray and Bill, the other paramedic on duty, dodged and lunged their ambulance through early rush hour traffic, sirens blaring. A police car arrived just as they did. The police quickly blocked off the sidewalk with their car and began moving bystanders away.

Bill backed in over the curb and Ray jumped out with his kit. Two bodies. The first was a young black girl, red sneakers, shot through the chest. Dead.

A black teenage boy lay by the wall close by, basketball shoes, plaid shirt, Creed headband, shot in the upper chest and arm. Leg twitching. Pulse: light and fast, respirations gasping. It was Clyde.

Ray put a tourniquet on his arm above the wound to stem the bleeding. Bill came over with the gurney and they hoisted him onto it. Sonny pushed through the crowd and bent over his brother. "My God! They shot Clyde. Is he dead?"

Ray hastily set up an IV on the other arm. "No. Alive."

Sonny shouted, "I *told* Clyde not to wear my headband. Oh s___! What can I do? What can I *do*?"

A policeman came over and restrained him. Ray found a vein and got the needle in. "Pray for Clyde." He glanced up. "You can pray for him, Sonny. It will help a lot."

"But I..." Sonny looked desperate. "I've never prayed before. God wouldn't listen."

Ray hung the little IV bottle up in the gurney stand and the fluid began to flow. "Sonny, just start. God really loves first timers. Trust me."

Bill had been cutting off the shirt around the chest wound, mopping the blood with gauze and checking the heart beats. Sonny began to cry out. "Oh God please don't let my brother die. Please God, *please!*"

Grandma Helen blasted through the barricade, took a look at Clyde and wailed: "Just tell me! Is he *dead*?"

Sonny stepped in front of her and the policeman released him. "No, Grandma. They're fixing him up. He'll be okay. You'll see."

Helen grabbed Sonny by the shirt, glancing from his desperate expression to the paramedic bent over Clyde. She looked skyward. "Oh, Dear Lord, save this family. I can't do this alone."

She suddenly thrust Sonny to one side and lurched toward Clyde screaming so loudly the whole block froze. She tore the headband off Clyde and waved it at Sonny. "This! *This,* is what killed your brother! Did you give it to him?"

"No, no, I told him not to…"

Helen threw it on the ground and stamped on it over and over. "*Damn* those gangs. Damn…(gurgle)" She clutched her chest and flopped to the pavement, face down, lifeless.

Bill and Ray popped Clyde's gurney to the elevated position and Ray fell on his knees to check Helen. "Bill, slip him in the van and get the paddles."

Ray called, "Sonny help me turn grandmother over." Not breathing. No pulse. Chest compressions started. Bill came charging back. "Defib charged up, Bill?"

Sonny flattened himself against the building, biting his index finger. "Oh no. Oh *no!*" He stared down at them, twitching each time the defibrillator convulsed his grandmother.

Bill dashed back in the ambulance to check on Clyde. Ray looked up at the boy whose face asked the question. Ray shook his head as tears streamed down Sonny's cheeks. He stood up and held Sonny in his arms.

Two policemen moved close to them with curious expressions. One said, "Coroner's on his way. He a relation?"

Still holding the boy, Ray turned to them. "This is Sonny. His only relations are his brother in the van and this is his grandmother. He has no parents and there's a younger sister at home. Call Child Services, okay?"

The policeman nodded. "You got it."

Ray released Sonny but spoke close to his face. "I'm taking Clyde to the hospital now, but there will be someone here to take care of you and your sister soon. I'll see you tomorrow."

Sonny gave a quick nod of understanding. "You did nothing wrong. Okay?" Ray dashed to the van and closed the door. The sired wailed and they pulled away. Glancing back he saw Sonny through the crowd. He knelt beside his grandmother, holding her hand and praying.

TWO FOR THE HOSPITAL

Clyde had regained consciousness by the time they reached the Emergency entrance. He looked up at Ray sitting beside him. "Blades did it," he said with a hoarse voice. "I saw the red bands when they drove by. They just started shooting."

"We figured. How bad does it hurt?"

"Shoulder hurts when I breathe. Am I going to die?"

"Nope. You're going to live and brag about it to all your friends."

"You're no doctor." He coughed and winced. "How do you know?"

"Cause Sonny prayed for you."

Clyde started to laugh but winced. The van doors opened and Bill began to pull him out. Shortly they were behind pull curtains in the ER joined by a doctor and a nurse. Ray twisted his knuckles lightly over Clyde's forehead. "These guys are taking over. You hang tight, my man." They banged fists on Clyde's good side. "I'll check on you later."

Bill met him on the loading dock and shook his head. "What a way to end a shift. Think I'll stop at the Bright Lights bar on my way home. Wanna come?"

"Another time, maybe. You take the van back without me. I've got another patient to visit."

Ray went to the floor where "Miss Comfort" was staying and found her nurse at the station. "Ah, Mister Johnson, you signed her in so, like it or not, you're her temporary guardian."

Ray returned a gritted-teeth smile. She said. "I'm Evelyn. Kitten, or whatever is her real name, is due for release tomorrow. She has a badly sprained wrist but no clear signs of a concussion. Still, the doctor wants her to go where she can be observed for at least 24 hours."

"Well, she's sure not coming home with me."

Evelyn suppressed a smile with tight lips. "I understand. We've arranged for a juvenile home to take her, but we'll need your signature."

"Juvenile home?"

"I guess you don't know her age or anything more about her, do you, Mister Johnson?" Ray shook his head. "Doctor Moore believes she is between 14 and 15. The oral surgeon concurs. She's got some big cavities, by the way."

"The girl didn't give you any history?"

"She told us she just fell down. Beside that, the only word she says is 'no.' Her doctor got our ethics person to allow opening her fanny pack in the personal effects locker, but it had no real information."

No IDs?"

"No. Well, a totally fake NYU student ID showing her name as 'Kitten Crawford', age nineteen."

Evelyn motioned for him to move away from the others in the nurse's station. She lowered her voice. "The pack contains mouthwash, pepper spray, a negligee, lipstick, condoms and four hundred dollars in cash." She sighed and rolled her eyes at the ceiling.

Ray thanked her, signed the discharge paper and went to Kitten's room. Their patient was shaking her head and saying 'no' to a slim young woman in a beige suit. He walked up between them. "Hello, Kitten."

The girl didn't smile, but stopped scowling and made eye contact with him. The woman in beige shook his hand with a big smile. "You must be Mister Johnson. I'm Suzanna Clark. I've been telling Miss. Kitten about a place to stay. Could I have a word with you in the lounge after your visit?"

"Uh, sure."

Kitten watched Suzanna leave but did not speak until the door closed. "Ray, that lady's been trying to talk me into some

Christian lockup and hopes you'll go along. I'm not a victim and it's not happening, okay?"

"No one will try and force you to do anything and the juvenile home is just for a few days after the hospital. They treating you okay?"

"Food's good. Got some Percocet for my wrist, but I gotta get out of here for something better."

"Listen, Kitten, you're getting discharged tomorrow. They need to watch you for any late signs of concussion for a few days at least."

"Been there before. Been worse places. Ain't gonna stay long."

"I've been praying with Winnie and Sophie for your recovery."

Kitten made brief eye contact but dropped her gaze to chest level, her face expressionless. "Look, Ray, thanks for helping me. I owe you, so I'll do you for free. You name the place."

He chuckled. "Thanks, but I'm trying my best to avoid sex before marriage. Don't feel you owe me anything."

"Yeah, I do. If you're gay, I can arrange that too, or are you just a square bear?"

"Whatever that means--oh, wait." Ray's jaw dropped. "I just remembered. Winnie said, 'I'd give anything to get that girl to go to church just once. Kitten, you don't know, but that old woman is dying of cancer. You want to do something for me? Let's go to church for her."

"Aw, 'c—p'. Religious stuff." She stuck out her tongue. "Okay, but if I do go just once, we're all even right?"

"Absolutely. Let's say a week from this Sunday at nine. Be at Winnie's then, or I can pick you up at the youth shelter if you're still there."

"Yeah, sure. On your way out, ask the nurse if I can have another pain pill, okay?"

Suzanna got up from her chair as Ray approached. She greeted him, asked to have their talk outside, and led him to a small garden courtyard in the back of the hospital. "Some of what I'm going to say isn't for public consumption."

"Look, Suzanna, whatever this is about, make it quick. I'm off duty and it's been a tough day. How'd you find out about her anyway?"

"Sophia called me. I gave a talk about human trafficking at her church and asked for anyone to alert us if they hear about a girl in distress."

"Sophia, huh."

"Ray, I'm with a Christian group dedicated to rescuing girls from the traffickers. We coordinate with others fighting for CSEC victims."

"CSEC?"

"Oh, sorry. That stands for 'Commercial Sexual Exploitation of Children.' We operate a residential facility called 'Saveher Ranch.' It's located in a wooded area in southern Pennsylvania."

Ray puffed his cheeks and blew out a breath. "If you think I can talk that girl into going with you, Suzanna, you're wasting your breath."

She bestowed a patient smile. "Of course not, Ray. Most of our girls turn it down at first. They are psychologically trapped into service by their captors and drugs. You might call it brainwashed. It seems strange to outsiders, but they have a weird loyalty, even a distorted love/ fear relationship for the pimp who manages them. The girls call him their 'boyfriend' and hope he'll protect them, but some pimps turn 'gorilla' on misbehavers and beat them anyway."

"You make it sound like a Nazi prison camp."

She nodded. "There are some similarities, but rather than being just captured, they are coerced, or romanticized into joining. Every human being has an inner desire to belong, and the criminal organization does give them that—same for gangs."

"So, why don't you locate their relatives or place them in foster homes?"

"The foster home system is severely broken. At this point in their lives, most girls wouldn't stay anyway. Just like four out of five people in prison, they've been in foster homes already.

These kids are brainwashed to return back to the organization partly because they have such low self esteem and they feel dependent on the drugs they supply."

"But you're offering them a much better life."

"Yes, it seems strange, but, as I said, they're used to the syndicate giving them structure in their lives and drugs. To get them back into the community the girls need to learn social and life skills, and, most importantly, they need to discover a loving Jesus. At the Saveher Ranch we develop an individualized long term treatment plan for each girl."

Ray tossed his head back. "Whoa, sounds amazing, but I never heard of you guys. So every girl gets her own program, huh?"

"The Lord made every one of us unique, Ray." Suzanna smiled. "But can you guess what every one of our underage prostitutes at Saveher Ranch has in common?"

"Tattoos?"

Ignoring his attempt at humor, her gaze became penetrating, her voice strained. "They've never had a good and steady father at home, Ray. So far I've worked with hundreds of these girls and, sadly, I've personally never met one who had a reliable father. Don't misunderstand. Many children are raised well by strong mothers who carry the load themselves, even sent their kids to Harvard. It's just been my experience that none of the girls in our program have good fathers at home."

"If you're thinking I'll adopt her, I'm not even married."

That got a brief smile. "Please be serious. All I'm asking for is a little cooperation. At the moment we are working on identifying our girl and learning about her background. Our immediate goal is to make sure she at least knows about another way of life, and a life with a Father in Heaven as well."

"Yeah, I remember Pastor Will saying God is the father to the fatherless."

"Absolutely, and we arrange introductions. Look, in the future, if the girl makes any contact with you…" Suzanna handed him a card. "Please call us."

"But you know she'll be right there in that youth shelter."

"She won't stay there, Ray."

PIPE BREAK

Two days later, Ray had just taken the Shrimp Alfredo out of the microwave when his doorbell rang. He squinted through the peephole at a smiling face below a uniform cap. "Who is it?"

"Al's Plumbing, sir. The Super sent us up. There's a leak in the ceiling below you. Like to check the tub drain. Won't take a minute."

Ray shrugged. "Sure."

He began to open the door slowly but found himself being pushed back by a tall burly man holding an eighteen inch length of pipe. "Uh, hello. Bathroom's down that hall on the right." Ray focused on the pipe. It was a three quarter-incher with an end cap screwed on giving it the heft of a steel club.

The man had a three day beard, a skull tattoo on his arm and smelled of sweat and cologne. He just grinned at Ray's face for a moment watching the color drain out. Another man, sporting a shoulder holster, entered and took a position behind Ray. The big guy tapped his pipe into the other hand. "You can call me Ernie. You're Ray Johnson, right?"

"Yes," he squeaked. "You're not plumbers, are you?"

Big guy's look turned condescending. "Course we are, Ray. We fix leaks in our system."

The second man tapped Ray's shoulders from behind. "Hands up."

Ray's arms shot to vertical. "Wallet's on my bedroom dresser." He began to tremble. "It's all the cash I have--honest."

The man patted him down. "He's clean."

Ernie frowned. "Not rollin' you, Bud. She's in here, right?" He gave Ray's arm a swat with the pipe.

"Ow. I..." His brow furrowed. "I haven't had a 'she' in here since I moved in."

Ernie thumb-gestured to his companion. "Have a look around."

The background noise became slamming closet doors and drawers falling out. Ray pleaded, "Just tell me who you're looking for. Maybe I can help you."

"Ah, you act so innocent. We know you've been dippin' into Kitten out of school, and now she's dropped out of sight. She's ours, Pal, and lots of the regulars are asking for her. You can't keep her for a pet—not without broken bones, understand?"

Ray guarded against another blow, but Ernie hit the other arm backhanded. He was real good with the pipe.

"Ow. S__t." He rubbed the sides of his arms. Ray's mouth dropped open with sudden realization. "Kitten! Of course. She was knocked unconscious a few days ago. I'm a paramedic. I patched her up and took her to North General. I think they released her to a juvenile facility somewhere."

Ernie looked thoughtful. He called out, "Mickey, check his wallet. The guy says he's a medic."

The man came back in a moment holding the wallet open to Ray's badge. "Yeah, he is, and there's no sign of our lady."

Ernie squinted. "But if *that* happened, she would'a called."

"Unconscious and taken to the hospital, Ernie. Her cell phone was smashed."

Ernie pointed a sausage finger at Ray. "We got you making three trips back to Kitten's shop."

"Not to *her* apartment, Ernie. I'm a Hospice volunteer for Mrs. Garcia next door. That's why I treated Kitten in the first place."

Mickey was on his cell phone, but put it back in his pocket. "North General had a Kitten Crawford. Discharged."

Ernie released a string of profanity. "We got a bum tip, Mickey." Turning to Ray, he dropped the arm holding the pipe and smiled. "Sorry about that, Pal. I owe ya a make up. We got a reputation to do good for our customers."

"I'm not a customer."

"Or the uniform. Anyway, you know Al's Bar and Grille on East 110th?"

"Yeah, I do. Picked up a fight victim there a few months ago."

Ernie's big chest bounced with his chuckle. "That's the place. Well, if you ask the bartender for a 'Maggie's special', you'll get a freebie on me. Enjoy."

Ray grinned. "That's very generous of you, Ernie, but could I trade it for another favor instead?"

"Maybe. What?"

"When Kitten shows up, how about you forgive her this time and don't beat her up? That sound okay with you?"

Ernie's great head and eyebrows lowered into an intense glare. He began to tap the pipe in his hand again. "Wait, so you *do* know the little lady."

Ray bit his lip then steadied his voice. "Nah, but look, Ernie, I'm a busy man. You'll save me from having to cart her broken bones back to North General again."

Ever so gradually, Ernie's scowl morphed into a grin, and he released a heaving belly laugh. He poked Ray in the chest with his pipe. "Oh, yeah. Sure." He turned to Mickey. "Get it?"

"Uh huh. Like protection money?"

Ernie gave Ray a tap on his arm, a gentle one this time, and headed for the door. "You got it, Pal."

WHO, ME?

Ray sat in Pastor Will's office whistling to himself and bouncing one leg. Will came in with a stack of books, closing the door behind him with one foot. "Sorry I'm a little late, Ray, but I had to work this meeting you wanted between some other things."

Ray coughed. "I won't take much of your time."

Will put the books down and sat on his desk, leaned back on it and faced Ray. "Take all the time you need. We missed you at our Comfort Zone meeting the other night. Lots of great witnesses."

"Had to work. Listen, I'm dropping out of the program— at least after I'm finished with this one lady. I'm just not the kind of man to handle what's been coming down here."

The pastor studied Ray's face for a moment, slipped off the desk and walked to a side table. "Coffee?"

"No thanks."

Will took a cup for himself and returned to sit in a chair to be at eyelevel with Ray. "You see a hospice patient twice a week, right? Tough to see someone die?"

Ray blew out with his cheeks. "No, if that were all, I'd stay with it. Sure, I've gotten to know Winnie and I hate to see her getting sicker, but that's not it."

Will allowed for a space of silence, took a sip of coffee and put it down on the desk beside him. "Jeanine told us at last night's meeting she was bored with hospice work, but each patient is different so she's staying with it."

Ray chortled. "*Boring*? Here's the thing. I got involved treating a prostitute who got heaved against a wall and with people who victimize them. Do you know she's only 15 at most? I also tangled up with two black boys being recruited by the Creed gang. I treated them to a visit at the firehouse, but later one was shot, and their grandmother was so upset she died on the street right in front of me."

Wide-eyed and open-mouthed, Pastor Will threw his head back. "Wow. That's awful. Some kind of *record*. The Lord sure has plans to put you to work."

"Look, I didn't sign up for this, Pastor. Grandma Helen was the only support for these kids. Sure, I could leave them in Child Services, but I don't want to. Now I have this *feeling* inside, I…"

"We know that feeling well, Ray." Will nodded. "It's a calling, sort of an anointing from the Lord."

"I don't want it!" Ray scowled. "I'm not equipped to help teenagers. There should be government agencies for this sort of thing."

"There are." Still grinning, Will shrugged. "And you can just walk away."

Ray dropped his head and gazed at the floor for another moment of silence. "But what—what can I do to make this thing, this *ache* inside of me go away?"

"Oh *that*." He laughed. "I'm afraid you're stuck with the ache. Everyone in His service gets it. Sorry, but it won't leave and only gets worse. *However,* if you give in and follow your new calling, I promise you it will be replaced with joy."

"New *calling*!?"

"Yep, when you went out of the comfort zone you dropped into the blessing zone. The good news is God will be at your side doing the heavy lifting for you. This church will help you too, if we can."

"You know you haven't been any help so far."

"Did you ask? We'll start with prayer, and I'll put you in touch with a man who works with youth gangs. I also know of a band that plays concerts to change the minds of trafficked victims. Maybe you can get your girl and her friends to attend."

"My girl? Doesn't sound like you're taking my resignation."

"Not mine to grant." He pointed his finger. "Ray, before this happened, what did you do with your free evenings?"

"Watched sports and sitcoms mostly."

Pastor Will laughed.

CLYDE

The receptionist smiled at Ray. "Clyde Jackson is in room 509, the pediatric floor. It's not quite visiting hours but I won't split hairs with a paramedic."

He blew her an air kiss and she added, "Oh, and Doctor Delgado is rounding. He can tell you more than I know."

Ray was familiar with most of the hospital personnel and had no difficulty finding him. The doctor saw him coming and waved him over. "I'm glad I caught you. We had to tell Clyde about his grandmother this morning and he's taking it pretty hard. Any familiar face would help."

"I'll do my best, but how is he medically?"

"He's a lucky boy. The bullet that went through his arm and nicked the brachial artery. Your tourniquet held his blood loss and I repaired the vessel. His chest wound is another matter."

"Still critical?"

"Quite the contrary. Our thoracic surgeon was amazed. The bullet passed between his ribs, front and back and somehow missed his lung. Seems impossible for a bullet pass through a body and do so little damage. If there's no change or infection in another three days, we'll let him go."

"To the juvenile facility?"

"Right. With his brother and sister. "

Clyde lay with his right arm in a suspension sling, his face tear-streaked. He looked up at Ray and gave a quick wave of recognition with his left hand. Ray's expression showed his concern, but he insisted on a fist bump before he sat on the bedside chair. "Real sorry about your grandma, Clyde."

Clyde's voice was soft and scratchy. "Was she shot too? They won't tell me."

"No, no. Heart attack, probably from the shock. She was pretty sick already. No one's fault, Clyde."

He blinked hard, lay back on the pillow and went silent. Ray asked about his pain but got no answer. "Clyde, has Sonny been by to see you?"

Clyde pouted. "Ya hafta be eighteen or someone with you. Anyway they got him and Hattie locked up somewhere."

Ray chuckled. "Not locked up, Clyde. They're in a group home and you'll be joining them soon."

"Oh, whoopee. Anything else you gotta say, I..." Suddenly Clyde sat up off the pillow, looking past Ray. He flashed a big white smile. "Hi, Mister Scott."

Tom Scott was approaching with an older boy. Tom began to lurch side to side. "Hey, now. What trouble you got yourself *into*, boy?"

Clyde sat up fully. "I got shot, Sir."

"Do tell." Tom flopped his head side to side and gestured to the boy next to him who gave Clyde a finger pistol-point. "This is my son, Andy. So, are we at war, or what?"

"Yeah, it was the Blades. They saw the Creed band on me and tried to pick me off. I'll get em later, though. They'll hafta pay for this."

"Vengeance is for the Lord, son." He swung a chair around and sat on it backwards facing Clyde. "But tell me, why do the Blades want to kill the Creeds?"

"They want what's west of Malcolm X Boulevard, but they ain't getting it."

Tom flashed a fake surprise look. "Really? The Creeds got title deeds to Manhattan? They must be really rich."

Clyde looked puzzled. "They, uh, it's rights. We fightin' for *rights.*"

Tom leveled his gaze and tone of voice. "Ah, rights..." He pursed his lips. "Rights to be drug dealing criminals and for selling girls to the syndicate. Think that's a cause worth dying for, Clyde?"

Clyde's head dropped. "I, uh..."

"We all get to make choices, son. On the other hand, you could choose to risk your life to save people." He thumbed at Ray. "Like this doofy white guy here. If he hadn't tied off your arm, you'd be pushing up daisies. Did you thank him for that?"

"Oh." He turned to Ray, his expression meek. "Thanks, Mister Johnson."

Ray grinned widely. "Hey, my pleasure."

Tom got up and twirled his chair to one side. "So they tell me you're eating up too much hospital food and they're kicking you out soon. What'll you do next?"

"Can I still go to that picnic, Mister Scott?"

Tom scowled. "Well, I don't know. See, we had to drop you from the batting order."

Andrew was chuckling under his breath but Tom kept his expression serious. "I'm trying to think of what you might do to help our team."

"I know how to keep baseball score, and, and I can draw. I could draw pictures of the players."

Tom did his best to suppress a smile, but it kept oozing out the sides of his mouth. "I didn't know that. I'd hate having to make someone be the score keeper, but if you do that, we'll have an extra player. And we'd love a team artist. Do you think you could draw the face of a batter right after Andy strikes them out?"

LOOKIN' GOOD

The fire crew were washing the paramedic van in the short driveway off the sidewalk. Jim began soaping up the windshield while Ray worked on the wheels. "So, Ray, where do you find all this mud in Manhattan?"

"Central Park, of course. Bill and I had to get a man off the lawn yesterday."

Tom had the hose. He was spraying off the suds and "accidentally" catching select buddies in the overspray. "Too weak to run across the park with the stretcher, Ray?" Squirt.

"Hey, watch that. No, gotta have our equipment close."

"Oh, really? I know that spot on the lawn." Another "careless" spray. "It's where the girls sun their legs."

Ray held his sponge, ready to fastball it. "Hey! Just because a few kids think you're a rock star now, don't get a swell head."

Jim came over with towels, and tossed one to everyone. "Rock star, nothing. I hear Tom's one of those landed estate owners now. Right Tom?"

"You mean my grandfather's farm?" Tom was on a stepstool working on the sides of the van. "Gonna be more trouble than its worth, I think. Grandpa couldn't work it for his last few years before he died and left it to me."

Jim threw his hands in the air. "Well, its gotta be worth *something,* man."

"So far, all I have is a bill for the property tax. I had two realtors look at it and the news isn't good." He got off the stepstool and tossed the towels into a bucket. "There's not much market for small family type farms, even those in full operation."

Ray slid the towel bucket to one side. "But, Tom, if there's a house there and its paid for, you should be able to salvage some cash."

"Maybe, but I'll bet it will take me at least a year to get it in shape to sell. Anyway, I'm going to drive out to Jersey on Saturday and take a look."

Ray said, "Well, I love farms. I spent my early years on one, you know." He snapped his towel at Tom. "Say, why don't you ask some of your new groupies if they want to be hired hands? They'll be at our annual picnic in two weeks."

"Well, I'll be…" Tom folded up the stepstool. "You only *look* stupid, Ray. That's a great idea. I'd never get a days work out of my kids, and I bet those boys have never seen the country."

Ray took a few steps back to survey the van. "Say, good job, guys. She's looking real pretty." He raised a finger toward Tom. "Here's another great idea. You need to have an ex-farmer take a look at your place and give his opinion. I'd be glad to go with you on Saturday if you want."

Tom looked puzzled. "You'd really drive out to the place with me? It's way up on the New York-Jersey border, about two hours from here."

"For a couple of days, why not. I'm getting sick of all this concrete."

"Let's get one thing straight, though." He pointed a finger at Ray. "If you're looking for a consulting fee, I'm only paying minimum wage."

Ray laughed. "No cash needed, Tom, but you could pay me with one of your wife's special meatloaves when we get back. One of those would feed me for a week."

#   #   #

The George Washington Bridge faded out behind them as they trusted their Garmin Navigator to find the best way to Route 23 and find their made up address in Colesville. Ray chuckled. "This thing has no idea about RFD routes. I hope you'll remember those farm roads when we get close, Tom."

"No sweat, but if you see a 'Welcome to New York or Pennsylvania' sign, we missed it."

"You're so encouraging. Can I ask you something personal?"

"Ask away."

"How come your grandfather left the farm to you instead of your dad?"

"Well," Tom let out a breath. "I guess because Dad didn't need the money, and also because they didn't get along for some time. My father is a professor and he lives in Boston now. My sister lives there, too."

"Did they argue or what?"

"First, let me say that I love my Dad, and he and mom did a good job of raising me. They traveled a lot, though, so I spent a lot of time with my grandparents while my sister, Emily, usually went with her other grand mom in Boston. The biggest problem was my farmer grandpa had a whole different idea about God. Didn't sit well with Dad."

"This is getting interesting." Ray pointed to one side. "Ha! Now there are as many cows as houses. We must be getting closer. So, your Dad doesn't believe in God?"

Tom shot Ray a furrowed brow glance. "Didn't I tell you he's at a university? Unless it's Christian, the culture there insists that man is the only intelligent life and is in charge of the universe."

Ray laughed. "Oh yeah, and it's not funny. I've heard they rewrote the old history books. Our kids are being taught that the devout Christians who founded America were really atheists and we need to scrap our country for a globalist, socialist world government."

"With them in charge, of course." They laughed. "Grandpa pointed out that all such governments have failed and ours only endured because of its biblical principals. He helped me to fully accept Christ in my heart."

"Yeah, and you turned out to be a great dad, too. Those street kids love you—they'd probably work for free just to hang out with you."

"Really?" Tom snortled. "I could write a whole book on the mistakes I've made as a father."

"Hey, maybe you really should."

"No way." He shot Ray a fiendish look. "Dads have to learn the hard way."

"I'm sorry about your folks, though. Remember, Jesus did say that belief in Him would split families. Do you still see your parents?"

"Oh, sure. We drive up there every Thanksgiving." He turned off on a narrow, patched up road. "They go away on Christmas."

"We must be close now, huh. *All* cows and no houses. You know, I've got relatives like that too. Discussions of religion and politics are off limits. I pray for them."

Tom hit the brakes. "Whoa, almost missed the driveway. It's so overgrown."

He turned off at a rusted mailbox in the shape of a crowing rooster and the van began a slow, bumpy trek up a narrow dirt drive. Ray leaned forward. "Is that the house? Seems a long way back against the woods."

"Yeah. There's over ten acres here. I can see I'll have to have this driveway graded. We should have electricity, though. I put it in my name."

The van bounced up to the two-story white frame house and stopped beside steps leading up to the porch and front door. "Ray opened the car door and looked up at the house. "It's gorgeous. Needs some love, but this is much bigger than I thought."

Tom grinned. "Yeah, a lot of memories here."

Ray gave the whole place a 360 look. "Your barn is a different story though. No paint and it's leaning to one side."

"I know. Grandpa said he bought a support timber for a brace inside but never got around to having it repaired."

"Like I said: needs lots of love."

Tom opened the tailgate. "I'm going to stow our gear and put our Millie's Kitchen dinner in a cooler place. Have a look around and tell me what your farmer instincts have to say about this place?"

A few minutes later, Ray was inside and marveling at the size of the living room. "So, here's my thinking. Your farm isn't the size Con Agra would buy, but I have a marketing idea. There's about seven acres good for corn or wheat. Advertise it as available *rental* acreage."

"A rental property?"

"No, rentable farm land. Income producing for the new owners without any work on their part."

"Interesting. Any other ideas?"

"Sure. After you paint the barn, it becomes a cool oversized garage."

Tom laughed. "So, if you can't fix it, feature it, but we have another problem to solve. No water."

"I'm sure you're on well water. Where's your basement?"

Tom took him to the stairs but said, "Actually, I've never been down there."

"Yeah, well we better get the water going. I'm getting hungry."

Ray found the swinging light bulb and they stepped down into the cool damp cellar. "At least it has a concrete floor." He pointed to a large tank in the corner. "There's your water tank. The pump pressurizes it so you can take a shower upstairs." He pointed to a smaller tank. "And here's the hot water."

"Do you think the well is dry?"

Nope. See those two switches? Flip em both on."

When Tom did so the pump went on and Ray said, "Voila. See, when there's no one home, it's best to keep it turned off." He pointed to some wooden racks on the opposite wall. "Now there's something interesting. I see your Grandpa used to age wine down here."

"That's right. I remember he usually had some with dinner, but those racks look empty."

Ray was on his knees squinting into the openings. He reached way in and pulled out a dust covered bottle. "But here's one forgotten soldier, Tom."

Tom shook his head. "I've got a trash bin filling up by the back door."

Ray headed back up the steps. "Maybe trash, maybe not. This is one of those few things that improve with age."

"Okay, your call. I'll warm up our dinners in the microwave."

Ray turned on the sputtering water in the kitchen sink and washed off the bottle. "It's a California cabernet, twenty years old."

Tom found wine glasses in the cabinet and washed them. Ray already had a corkscrew in action and a moment later he was swirling the purple liquid in the glass. He gave it a sniff, then a sip. "Oh, my God, it's wonderful."

Tom set the dinners on the kitchen table and Ray handed him a wine goblet. "A toast to your new country estate." Ray chuckled. "This is from your grandfather, welcoming you as the new owner. I bet he's smiling at us right now."

They clinked and sipped. Ray lifted his glass. "May the Lord bless this home and the next family who comes to live here."

CHURCH

Winnie wouldn't listen to any objections. She was coming with them and that's that. Ray and Sophie managed to heft her into the passenger seat of Sophie's car. "Look, grandma, we don't really know what to expect from this kind of person. Suzanna said that trafficked girls can be very paranoid. She might run off at the first stoplight or not even come with us."

"Kitten promised, didn't she?" Winnie asserted. "But look, if the girl bolts, we'll still enjoy a nice service at your church."

Ray called from the back seat, "She's not dangerous, guys, but she's got quite a mouth on her. I just hope she behaves in there. Suzanna advised we just treat her like we would any friend."

"Really?" Sophie chuckled as she steered into the parking lot at the youth shelter. "Our church is big on evangelism. I'm sure that girl's gonna hear something she won't like, but I did buy her some respectable clothes to wear for today."

"And I paid for her dental work. I think she'll behave. Paranoid or not, she ought to know by now we're not the enemy, and I can tell she respects Winnie."

Kitten was waiting for them in the reception area wearing Sophie's "church clothes" but in full scowl. Sophie decided Ray should drive so Kitten would be in the back seat between her and Winnie's folding walker. As they were getting in, Sophie made the mistake of saying, "I really hope this changes your life, Kitten."

"What the f___." Kitten's eyes blazed. "If you think I need your d___ Jesus, you're sadly mistaken, sister." She gave Sophie the finger. "I'm just fine, thank you."

"You don't have to go if you don't want to."

"I promised, didn't I?" Kitten got in the car. "I can sit through anything for an hour." She leaned forward. Her voice softened. "Ray, thanks for the dentist, but don't think that counts for another day in church."

They drove in silence for awhile. Kitten turned to Sophie and hissed. "So, Ray visited me the other day. He says Winnie told him your Dad's a real creep."

Winnie shrieked. "I did not! I just said he was absent most of the time."

"Yeah, like I said."

Sophie's face was pained. "He's really not so awful, just too busy for us. Kitten, what would you do, if *your* father showed up one day?"

Kitten looked like she was about to scream, but after a moment, her expression went flat. "I'd hire two goons to beat him to a pulp. No, you know what? Forget that. I really don't care. I'd just walk right past the bastard."

"Really," Sophie chuckled. "I might not be so extreme, but maybe we have something in common after all." She leaned forward and put her hand over the front seat. "Ray, there's the church. Turn into that parking lot."

Morningside Heights with its colleges and seminaries was more suburban looking than most of Manhattan. Sophie's church was set back and had trees and planters in the side yards with flowers leading up to the front door. While Ray assisted Winnie up the wheelchair ramp, Kitten and Sophie walked up a flight of stone steps and waited for them in the entrance courtyard. They tried to talk Kitten into sitting up front near the band, but that didn't go well.

Meanwhile, worshipers of all colors and ages were making their way in. One man carried his young son on his shoulders, spinning him around and laughing. Next to him, his wife was kneeling beside their seven year old daughter, fixing a bow in her hair. When she finished, she kissed her smiling child on the forehead.

Suddenly, Kitten collapsed on a bench and began to sob loudly. Sophie came and stood next to her. Winnie sat down beside her. "Kitten, what happened? What's the matter?"

She couldn't answer but pointed at the family. Sophie shook her head. "Those people, Kitten? What's the problem?"

Still pointing, Kitten croaked, "They're beautiful. They're just f___g *beautiful.*"

The little girl avoided her mothers attempt to restrain her, rushed over to Kitten and stood right against her knees, facing her. "You're thad," she lisped.

Kitten struggled to see through her tears. She shook her head, "no."

"Yeth you are. I'm Kali. What's your name?"

"My name?" She wiped her eyes on her sleeve and cleared her throat. She answered in a loud whisper. "My name's Rachel." Sophie's eyebrows went up.

Kali took both hands in hers and stood up straight. Her mother was about to seize her, but Sophie put out her arm. Kali announced, "I know how we make thad people happy again, Rachel. Okay if I pray for you?"

Her face relaxed in peace. She studied the earnest little evangelist and nodded.

"God knows why you are thad. Let Him inthide you and He will make you all better." She looked skyward. "Dear God, please tell Rachel you love her forever and make her all better. Amen."

Rachel drew her face close to Kali's and smiled. "You don't have any front teeth, do you?"

"No, but God will give them back." She produced a toothless grin that made Rachel chuckle.

"Well, Kali," She sniffed and wiped the remaining tears away with a finger, "I feel better already. Thank you."

"There. Thee? God can do anything." Kali gave Rachel a hug before an apologetic mother led her away.

Rachel looked up at Sophie with a pained expression. "Sorry, but I don't think I can go in there."

Sophie turned to Ray who had been watching in awe. "Tell you what. You and Winnie go into the main sanctuary. I'll go up the side stairs with our guest. We'll watch from the balcony. It's private up there.

Winnie wheeled in closer and put her hand on Rachel's arm. "We'll meet you back here after the service, Dear. You have a lovely name."

When the service was over, Rachel's expressionless face had returned. Winnie insisted on sitting in the back seat next to her. "Well, Dear, that wasn't *too* bad, was it?"

"No, but we're even now, right Granny?"

"Of course, but there never was a score to settle. Did you like anything at all about our service?"

After a silent moment she mumbled, "Music was okay."

Winnie slowly raised her hands. "Oh yes, I just *love* worship music." She moved closer to Rachel and lowered her voice. "Do you think God is real?"

Still with a deadpan expression and voice. "I'm hoping…" They bounced through a pothole. "not."

"Do tell. Humor an old lady. What would be the problem?"

She relaxed back on the seat and studied Winnie's face. "Lady, if I started listing the things I'd never be forgiven for, you'd have a heart attack. If there's really a God, he'll flick me onto His barbeque pit when I die."

Ray spoke to Sophie who was driving. "Left on Eighth Ave, then one more block up as I recall."

Winnie tapped Rachel's arm. "If you learn to trust in Jesus, I promise that'll never happen."

There was no response. Sophie turned and glanced into the back seat. "Rachel, I know this might have been a lot for you today, but Ray and I are coming by at noon on Wednesday. Suzanna might come, too. We can go out together, enjoy lunch and just chat about anything you want, okay?"

Rachel leaned forward. "Who the f___ told you my name?"

IN THE GAME

It was a beautiful day for the annual fireman's picnic: big white puffy clouds, balmy June temperature and boats sailing the East River. Who cares if you had to look past streams of honking cars on the FDR Drive to see the water. This was country in the city.

As promised, Ray brought Sonny, Clyde and their sister Hattie. Tom, now the coach, was busy organizing the baseball dugout with his boys, but as soon as he saw Ray, he waved for his wife and daughter to join them.

Tom began the introductions. "This is my oldest, Andrew. He's eighteen and starting City College in the fall." He lunged for and missed grabbing another son who hurried over to a pile of softball bats. "That's our second boy over there, who's about to be scolded. His name is Glen, and he's picking out his home run bat. Has to be just the *right* one, you know."

Ray gestured to his guests. "This is Sonny. He's fifteen going on twenty one, and here's Clyde, our resident artist and score keeper."

Tom's wife put her hand on her daughter's shoulder. "Hi. I'm Mona. This is Nevaeh, but you can call her Nevie. Please understand if she gets confused as to who's the mother in this family."

Nevaeh looked up at her, the whites of her eyes showing. "Mona, you know we talked about that."

Mother laughed. "She's ten."

Ray turned around quickly and brought the girl standing behind him to the front. She stood silently looking at the ground. "And, this is Hattie. She hasn't said much since her grandmother died, but we're really glad she's with us. I think she's ten as well, right Sonny?"

Sonny shrugged.

Tom opened his arms and herded all the boys toward the pile of equipment. "Time to get started. Sonny, can you catch fly balls?"

"No sweat, and I don't use a glove."

"No shame in using a glove, son. You can grab one anytime if you change your mind. You'll be in left field."

Glen asked, "Can I be at first base again?"

"Promised that to another, son. I put you at short stop. Don't worry, you'll be plenty busy. Meanwhile, you and Sonny start your warm up catches."

Andrew asked, "I'll be pitching again, right?"

"First seven innings. Michael's boy has been hurling some fast ones, so you'll get a relief this year." He waved at another boy. "Ah, here comes our catcher. Start warming up."

Andrew squinched his face. "I could pitch the whole game, Dad. Say, is our Chief gonna be the umpire again?"

"Nah, the Five Alarms cried foul last year. They got someone from the Mayor's office, but I don't know his name. Our Chief is over at the girls' game in the next field."

Clyde said, "I'm keeping score so where should I sit?"

"You, my friend, have the best seat: right behind the plate, and it looks like someone bought you a drawing pad and pencils as well as the score sheet." Clyde beamed.

Tom waved the team together. "Okay, men, check the batting order. Remember to be nice to these bums even if they don't deserve it." He put out his hands palms up and wiggled his fingers. "What's the word?"

Altogether they put their hands out like his and shouted, "Flames rule!"

Mona took the two girls with her into the bleachers. "Just listen to those men, would you. If you two would rather go over and watch the girls' game, we can."

Nevaeh gave her mother a disciplinary look. "Mother, you know our boys would be disappointed if we didn't watch them for a little while."

Mona smiled. "That's very thoughtful, Nevie."

They sat with Hattie between them. Nevaeh turned to her. "Are you in fifth grade, too?"

97

Hattie's head still hung down, but she gave a little nod.

Mona said quietly, "Nevie, it hasn't even been two weeks since her grandmother died. She may not feel like talking."

"Uh, huh." Nevaeh touched the back of Hattie's head. "Hattie, you only have *one* half tied pigtail back here and the other side is all frizz."

Hattie kept her head down but replied, "Grandma Helen was a fixin' them when she got called away."

Mona gasped and put her hand over her mouth. "Well! From two weeks ago?" She picked Hattie up and sat her on her lap. "Grandma would be so angry with us if we didn't finish up, wouldn't you say?"

"I guess."

While Mona got to work Nevaeh was reassuring. "Don't worry, Hattie; mother is real good at this."

Hattie reached into her dress pocket and pulled out a red rubber band. "I was holding this for her."

They looked up when the crowd cheered. Sonny hit a triple and waved at them when he reached the base. They waved back.

Nevaeh spoke in a motherly tone. "Now Hattie, we won't make you talk 'cause I imagine losing your grandmother was the *worst* thing that ever happened to you."

Hattie shook her head, "No."

Mona's eyebrows dropped. "No? Something even worse?"

Hattie nodded, "Yes."

They sat quietly for a moment to see if she wanted to say anything else. Hattie reached into another pocket and withdrew a rumpled newspaper clipping. "Sonny saved this."

Mona gently took the clipping and spread it out on her lap. It was a photo and caption. "Ah, this was the shooting scene. Of course! It was even worse because your brother Clyde got shot, right?"

Hattie shook her head, "No."

Mona read the caption. "Scene of the drive-by shooting on Monday afternoon. Clyde Jackson lies on the stretcher with a chest wound. Helen Jackson, his grandmother, is next to him with an apparent heart attack. The body next to her is a girl, the only one fatally shot in this incident. Name withheld pending notification of kin."

Hattie had begun to cry. She tapped the photo of the dead girl.

"Oh, my God." Mona put her hand over her mouth. "You *knew* her, didn't you? She was your friend?"

"Best friend." Hattie croaked.

Mona clutched Hattie to her and both sobbed while Nevaeh gave them reassuring strokes on their shoulders.

After a few minutes Hattie's sniffles subsided. Nevaeh supplied them both with tissue and proceeded to rub away their tears. She said, "Hattie, I think softball is *boring*. I say we go and explore this park, huh?"

Hattie glanced up at Mona. "Is it okay?"

"Well, yes, but don't get out of sight."

Nevaeh skittered to the end of the bleachers and jumped down, Hattie right behind her. "I know this park from last year. Gonna show you something real gnarly, girl."

Hattie's mouth dropped. "What?"

"Ain't tellin' yet."

Mona's hand covered her mouth, anxiety in her eyes as they walked away.

Nevaeh took Hattie's hand. "But first, mother gave me some money. Have you ever had cotton candy?"

Hattie shook her head. Nevaeh pointed her finger at her face. "We can share but no gobbling it down, okay?" They began to skip together toward the concession stands.

The crowd cheered again. Sonny ran over home plate with arms raised in triumph. Mona hardly noticed. She settled back watching the girls, a wide grin spreading over her face.

RACHEL

Ray glanced over at Sophie as he drove through Manhattan's streets. "I'm glad you found some free time to visit Rachel with me. I never know what to say, and she definitely relates better to women."

"Like I know some magic words? She'll talk to me but she's got a hard shell around her inner self."

"True, but remember how emotional she got when she saw that happy family on Sunday."

At the next light, a man with a briefcase hurried through the crosswalk as the light turned green. Ray had to stop short to avoid hitting him. The man scowled at him, slapped his palm on the hood and shouted. "Hey! Watch it, buddy."

"Careful," Sophie chuckled. "This isn't West Virginia."

"So Winnie squealed on that one too, huh?"

"Ray, did you say Suzanna might meet us at the youth shelter?"

"She did. Suzanna phoned me last night and said her investigation was almost complete. Hopefully, she's got Rachel's background story."

"Really." Sophie shook her head. "I'm guessing it's not pretty."

Ray turned down into the underground garage at the facility. "I'm not sure why we're spending all this time with her. Aren't the institutions supposed to figure out what to do with her? Besides, I'm not sure anything will change her."

"Nonsense." She pointed. "Look, there's a good parking spot. One thing at a time. Save the girl first. Change can come later."

"Hope you're right."

"Look, lets be patient and keep talking about God's love. There's always hope for anyone."

"Mentioning God turns her off. Sorry, but it looks hopeless to me."

As they headed up the stairs, Sophie rapped Ray on the shoulder. "You can be a quitter if you want, but I'm going to keep trying."

Suzanna was waiting for them in the lobby. She approached the couple with her hands raised. "Rachel's gone."

They slammed to a stop and spoke in unison. "What?" Sophie asked, "Wait, you mean they have her working somewhere?"

"Nope. She left last night. They sent her to empty some garbage and she never returned. Unfortunately, that's typical for these girls."

Ray shrugged. "So, that's it, then." He gave Sophia a 'told you so' look. "It's over."

Suzanna brushed back her long brown hair with one hand. "I hope not. Look, let's have lunch anyway. I want to tell you more about Rachel and our Saveher organization."

When they had settled into a corner table at a Burger King a block away, Suzanna continued. "Saveher has an agreement with authorities to trace down trafficked girls. Thanks for the information you gave me on Sunday. Confirming her name as Rachel was a help. Her last name is Clemmons. She was born in Jersey City fifteen years ago yesterday."

Sophie said, "So she left on her birthday."

"Yes, but I doubt she even remembers. Rachel's father was sent to a federal penitentiary when she was six. Her mother was an alcoholic and a drug user. She had various jobs and men came and went in her home. Some of the men abused Rachel while they were there."

Sophie pushed away her half-eaten burger. "That's so sad. Where's her mother now?"

"Died of an overdose just before Rachel's thirteenth birthday and the girl disappeared before Child Protective Services could take her in."

"Bummer." Ray sighed. "But why New York? Did she want to become a prostitute?"

Suzanna threw her head back. "Oh, my Lord, no. She thought she had an aunt in New York, but the relative left for parts unknown. The gangs here can spot stray girls and they pretend to be their saviors. Actually they sell them to the pimps working for the syndicate. Did you know this is a thirty billion dollar industry?"

Sophie said, "Good grief, but all she had to do was go to any police station."

"True, but most of these girls start with a mistrust of authorities and especially men. The traffickers have their own induction program to gain their trust. They'll often start with romancing them, but get them hooked on drugs and petty crimes so they will avoid the police. Soon, their only 'friend' is the manager or pimp they call 'boyfriend.' By then they are completely controlled."

"I just don't get it." Sophie slapped the table. "These are American girls. They must *know* there's a better life for them. Don't they just look around and see it?"

"It might be hard to believe, but they have such low self esteem the girls think they only deserve the captive life they have. They don't think of themselves as victims even though they are. The average victim we see returns back to their life eleven times."

Suzanna pointed a finger at Ray. "What you told me on the phone was interesting. That breakdown at the church points to a covered up, inner self. All these girls have a former self hidden under a hard psychological shell. You saw a peek underneath, but notice how her breakthrough personality disappeared a few minutes later."

Ray blew out through his cheeks. "Okay, I'm convinced. Like I said, it's hopeless. What are we even doing here anyway?"

That earned him a swat on the arm from Sophia. "Oh Ray, where's your faith? Suzanna's in the business of *saving* girls, not giving up on them." She opened her hand toward her. "Right, Suzanna?"

"Absolutely. Saveher has a large residential rehabilitation center in an isolated area. There is no confinement but it is twelve miles from any outside structure. We bathe our girls in Christian love. Beside room and board, they get to complete high school including sports and the arts. We provide them with medical and dental care as well. Most of our graduates eventually welcome God as the father they never had, and every time I see one girl come to the Lord, I feel I have the greatest job on Earth."

"But to *get* them there, you do what..." Ray opened his hands. "Drop a fishing net over them and speed them out of town."

Sophie pointed a thumb at Ray while she spoke to Suzanna. "He likes to think he's funny."

Suzanna was laughing. "If it weren't illegal on five counts, I'd consider it. Seriously, folks, it really is difficult, but there are a few who go voluntarily. Some are rescued by government agencies like Social Services, and others may be saved by the mother or other relatives."

Ray said, "Sorry if I was being flip. Assuming we locate her, do you have any plan in mind for Rachel?"

"I do. She has a warrant for her arrest for parole violation and Saveher has a liaison with the police. Normally we *never* release the names of the girls to police, but this is the exception. We'll start by having her arrested."

"But, Suzanna," Sophie squinched her face. "Isn't that cruel? She'll hate authority even more."

"Sophie, believe me, jail would be a step up from her lifestyle. However, she won't have to stay there. We have an agreement with the court to take custody of her for the duration of her jail time. It will be her choice, but so far, hardly anyone has turned us down."

"Great. How can we help find her. All the working girls look alike to me out there."

"Be alert and pray about it. You have me on speed call. If you can get Rachel by herself somewhere, I can have the police there pronto."

Sophie said, "We'll do our best, Suzanna." She turned to Ray and put her hand on his shoulder. This time, her grip was firm and gentle. "Would you like to pray with me?"

ROAD TRIP

Two adults and six adolescents squished into the seven passenger wagon and headed north out of Manhattan. The boys were singing rap songs with gusto while Hattie and Nevaeh ignored them with their newly-found, scowling togetherness. When the van began to rock side to side over the George Washington Bridge, Tom hollered for them to cool it. Later, the poking, expletives and cap stealing escalated. Tom suggested they might turn around. He used different words.

The entourage pulled into a rest area on the Garden State Parkway for gas and a little fatherly discussion. Mona, however, had the solution. She moved Andrew to the front seat so she could sit with the girls in the second seat and let the remaining boys wiggle around in the back. No more rap.

Mona discovered a problem as they pulled out on the road. "Oh, dear, there are only two seat belts in this seat."

Hattie slipped onto her lap and snuggled. "It's okay. If we crash, we can just hold on tight."

Nevaeh's look said, "Nice move, clever girl."

Mona took out a book from her bag. "All right, but this way, *you* have to be the one to read the story I brought."

Nevaeh realized right away this was really a reading lesson, so she began to report on all the interesting scenery they passed: "Look, bikers—oh, spotty cows—a convertible with the girl's hair flying around—a pink house."

The backseat boys discovered their mutual love of three handed pinochle and the inevitable question was left for all-by-himself Andrew. "How much longer before we get there, Dad?"

"About a half hour, Andy." Speaking into the rearview mirror, Tom called out, "Listen up everyone. We're stopping at Micky D's for dinner tonight. After that we do all our own cooking. There are four bedrooms upstairs but ours is on the first floor. Girls, you bunk in the first room on the left with the twin beds. Clyde, you and Glen get the one to the right with the bunk beds. Sonny and Andy get the two double beds. Questions?"

Nevaeh asked, "Can't anyone sleep in the fourth one?"

"Nope. That's a small room with grandpa's exercise equipment and books. Some of the books are for you guys, though. Check them out. Girls, you have the biggest room and I don't want to hear any complaints from the rest of you, okay?"

"Dad?"

"Yes, Glen."

"Is Grandpa's computer in there?"

"He never had one. No Internet or cell phone reception."

Groans all around. "But there is cable, so we do have TV. The new owners can get Internet that way, but for now, we're going to survive like it's the eighties again."

Nevaeh whispered in Hattie's ear. "My sleeping bag's full of games and stuff."

Hattie glowed with excitement. She whispered back, "Don't tell the boys."

Mona gave the girl on her lap a little squeeze. "And don't think I didn't hear that." They giggled.

Sonny called out from the back, "Mister Scott, what kind of work will we be doing?"

"Hoeing out ten acres by hand and slopping the pigs."

Andrew looked back at the stunned faces. With a grin he mouthed a silent, "No."

After a sufficient pause, Dad went on. "Actually, our big project will be painting the barn. I'll tell you about the other things tomorrow. Remember what I said. All the guys must work at least four hours a day before you can goof off. The Jackson work crew gets minimum wage. My kids get what I think they're worth when we're done. Understood?"

Andrew was still turned to face them. He made his voice deep. "And no mention of the child labor laws or you'll see the whip." Nevaeh was the only one who laughed.

Hattie looked up at Mona. "I don't think I can paint a barn, Mrs. Scott."

Mona chuckled. "Tom should have told you. The work you *girls* do will be with me. Nevaeh told me about your special talents."

Hattie bit her lip and shook her head. "Don't have those."

"That got a furrowed brow stare. "Oh really. And what were you and your friend planning when you finished school?"

Hattie's tongue appeared between her grinning teeth. "Open a bakery. I have all Grandma Helen's recipes saved."

"Uh huh, and how many is that?"

"Thirty five so far. My favorite is her molasses cookies with chocolate chips."

"You gettin' the idea, girl? We got eight hungry mouths to feed. Can you do biscuits, bread and rolls too? And what you gonna fix for dessert?"

Hattie began to bounce. "Oh, yes, yes. I can make *all* of those. Maybe tomorrow night I'll make a cherry pie, okay?"

"Well…" Mona gave her a squeeze. "I think that's more than okay. Nevaeh and I will be in the kitchen doing the main course and we'll all help each other. I also think we better hit the grocery store while we're in town."

FARM WORK

A van full of kids and Happy Meals pulled off the two-lane highway onto a dirt driveway. They bounced through ruts and puddles making their way through the overgrown fields toward the white farm house. The nearby gray barn, listed to one side, beckoning to the work crew.

"And here we are, folks. These fields once had crops and livestock. I'm hoping a potential buyer will see their potential, but don't try running across them. They're full of bumps and holes."

They pulled up to wooden steps that led to an expansive front deck. The only color was provided by three neglect-defying sun flowers beside the stairs. Mona called out, "Everyone get your things and carry them up to the porch. Dad has to get the electricity and water going, then we'll all take the gear to our rooms."

Tom carried their bags to the porch and disappeared into the house. Shortly, lights came on and he emerged. "It's almost dark, people, so no exploring out there until tomorrow, okay? Let's all meet in the living room when you're settled."

Mona and the girls were the last to join them since they had to put all the groceries away as well. She pouted at Andrew and Sonny who had commandeered the couch and were enjoying Cokes with their feet on the coffee table. "Comfortable? You look like you've been here all day." They both gave her a "thumbs up."

Tom brought a chair around in front of the fireplace to face everyone. He grinned. "Ah, this is so great. With all your help, we should have this place whipped into shape by the end of the week. Beside work, there are fun things to do around here and, we'll have plenty of time for them."

Clyde asked, "What could we do? Doesn't anyone live near here?"

"Good question. For one thing, we have kites and a badminton set. Also, Grandpa's good friends, the Marshals, live through the woods behind us. When you go over the hill, you'll see their place by the lake. I checked with Neil Marshal and you can use his canoes there."

Glen said, "Any kids?"

"Uh huh. They have two grandkids visiting for the summer, but they wouldn't interest you."

"Why not? Are they just babies?"

"No, they are only a year or so younger than you, Clyde, but they're both girls."

The whites of four boy-eyes flashed to the alert position. After a moment Glen tried out his most casual voice. "They black?"

"Yes, but why would that matter?"

Nevaeh threw her head back. "Oh, no, Hattie. We're gonna be the only ones left working." Laughter all around.

Next morning there was an enormous pan of eggs scrambled with onions and peppers, homemade biscuits and bacon. It disappeared in five minutes along with half gallons of milk and orange juice.

The girls headed out for badminton and exploration before the "lunch locusts" would return. Mother relaxed with coffee and her summer reading, stretched out on a chaise lounge she discovered on the side porch.

Tom gathered his troops in front of the barn. "All right men, our first job is to straighten this old girl up. Grandpa did put on a new roof a few years back but not before water rotted out one of the front cross braces." He pointed. "Andrew, get the van and back it up to right about here. We'll start by pulling this old girl upright."

"Glen, you and Sonny get the extension ladder around back and set it up on that cross beam while I get the rope."

Clyde looked up at Tom. "My arm's pretty good now. What can I do?"

Tom took him by the shoulders and grinned. "My boy, you might do more to sell this place than any of us. Mona knows where there's an easel and watercolors. Think you can do a painting of the house and barn? It would be a lot more effective than a photo in our sales ad."

Clyde's white teeth appeared. "Oh, can I *ever*. I'll have my barn painted before yours, and the house, too." He gestured to the porch. "I'll add missus Scott on the porch looking like a millionaire's wife and I'll put flowers in all them beds."

Tom tapped him on the back. "Sounds great. Now it's up to us to make the place look at least half as good as your painting."

The barn was eased to upright with the rope attached to the van. Sonny checked its position with level placed along its side and called out when the bubble was centered. Tom secured a new brace with lag bolts and the barn was straight by ten in the morning. Meanwhile, Glen had brought over two buckets of primer paint and brushes on extension poles. He said, "Dad, do you know what's under those tarps in the back of the barn?"

"Yup." He chuckled.

"Well, well..." He shook his hands. "What's under them?"

"They probably don't run, but there's a tractor and a jeep."

"Whoa," Andrew exclaimed. "If grandpa didn't farm, why'd he keep them?"

"The tractor has a road grader attachment for the dirt driveway, and if we have time we should give it a workout. The jeep has a snow plow, and he used it to run errands into town."

Sonny said, "Can we try and start em' up? I'll bet I can get them to run. I'm in the automobile tech course in school."

"No time right now. We have to get painting. Besides, I'd have to get fresh gas for them."

"So, we'll spend every day painting for the whole week?"

Tom laughed. "Nah, with four of us we should be done in a few days. Look, if we get two sides primer coated by one o'clock today, we'll take the rest of the day off."

"And do what?"

"Whatever you like. Maybe you and Andrew would like to take a look at those machines, and I know Glen and Clyde want to try out those canoes."

Smiles all around. "Grab your buckets. Let's get to work."

CHURCH SURPRISE

Sophia lingered after the church service to chat with friends about the sermon on forgiveness. They all agreed it was easy to talk about forgiving the unforgivable, but really hard to actually do it in real life. She walked out the front door into the June sunshine and was shocked to see Rachel, of all people, sitting at a side bench talking with Kali. Sophia walked around behind her where she could hear and pretended to study a handout.

Kali was saying, "I *told* you you'd feel better."

"I do. Thank you sweetheart." Rachel stood up and took Kali's hand. "Introduce me to your folks."

Her parents stood nearby, her younger brother trying to twist his hand out of dad's grip. Kali skipped over to them, Rachel in tow. "Rachel, this is my mommy and daddy."

Mother extended her hand. "I'm Lynn, and this is my husband, Ben. I hope Kali hasn't been bothering you."

"Nah, she's a good kid. You two are really in love, right?"

Lynn's head jerked back. "I, we—what kind of question is that?"

Kali had no trouble. "Oh, yeah. They're kissing *all* the time."

The little boy squirmed out of daddy's grasp and took off. Ben was snickering when he bent down to his daughter. "Go chase after him, Kali. Don't get lost." He straightened up and grinned at Rachel. "She's been telling you stuff about us, huh?"

Rachel's gaze went from one to the other. "Uh, no, not really. I was just watching you. Hope you didn't mind. You two look so, so *together*."

Understanding came across Lynn's face. She draped an arm over Ben's shoulders. "I'm the lucky one, Rachel. Don't settle for anything less than a God-fearing man."

Words weren't coming out from Rachel, so she continued. "You act like you're puzzled by us."

She shook her head. "Your husband—he really likes the kids, huh?"

Ben chuckled. "When I'm not ready to kill 'em. Hey, there's a singles bible study on Saturday mornings if you'd like to come: plenty of God-fearing young men showing up. In fact if they're not serious, we kick em out."

Sophia decided it was time to move in. "Ah, there you are, Rachel. I see you've met the Andersons." She smiled at them. "We better let them go find their kids before they do some serious damage. Can we do lunch?"

Rachel couldn't quite smile but gave a few quick nods toward the parents. "Real nice to meet 'cha."

Sophia waved at the Andersons. "Maybe see you on movie night, Wednesday?" She slipped her arm in Rachel's, turned around gently, and walked away.

"Didn't mean to butt in, Rachel, but we haven't had a chance to chat woman to woman. Did you enjoy the church service?"

"Nah. I wanted to see Kali and her folks. Where we going?"

"Out to lunch, just you and me."

She scowled. "You're really gonna take me back to that juvie home, aren't you?"

"Oh, no, I'm not. I promise. We're going to my place. It's only three blocks from here."

"Yer taking me to your house?"

"Well, yes, my condo, that is. I was planning to make some sandwiches and we can pick up soup from the deli downstairs. I'm an iced tea fan, but we'll get some sodas if you like."

She shrugged. "Sure."

On arrival, Rachel acted suspicious and looked in every room, but finally she relaxed against the patio railing. "Gee, you got a balcony with a view."

Sophia was busy in the kitchen area. "Yeah, it's only third floor, but you can see the Hudson and Jersey. Have a seat right where you are. Be ready in a minute."

She joined Rachel on the balcony with lunch on a tray. "When the weather is good and I have free time, I like to sit here and watch the ships go by."

Rachel slurped her soup down in half a minute. She began to eat aggressively and spoke with her mouth full. "You see Ray sometimes, right?"

"I do, usually at my grandmother's."

"Okay. Tell him thank you for the other favor he gave me when you see him."

"Of course. Mind if I ask what was the favor?"

"He got me a 'forgiveness pass' with my boss. I even got treated to a meal out."

"Oh," Sophia looked bewildered. "I'm glad that went well."

"You got a great place. Why are you both being nice to me?"

Sophia studied her for a moment. "I guess--I guess we want to show you there's another way of life, and, I'll admit, I'd like to talk with you about God, as well."

"Nothing wrong with my life, lady. I'm doing okay."

"Oh, Rachel, that didn't come out right. I just want us to be friends and talk about some things you might find interesting."

"No offense, but I got friends. You got a bathroom?"

She pointed the way. "Take your time. I'll fix some dessert."

"Okay."

When she left, Sophia grimaced and shook her head. She went to her bedroom and called Suzanna's number. "Hey, I got Rachel here in my apartment. I think I just ran out of things to say to her. Can you come over?"

Back in the living room, she called to the bathroom door. "Rachel, I have some scrumptious cupcakes out here if you're not full." Silence.

Sophia went to the bathroom door. "What would you like to do this afternoon? We could walk to the pier or see a museum, but maybe we should get you some comfortable shoes first."

No response from within. "And say, there's a street band that gives concerts on Sunday—I think I can already hear them in the distance." Silence.

Sophia rapped gently. "You okay in there?" She opened the door. Rachel was gone.

FRICTION

Tom and three boys had a good start applying the gray primer with wide brushes on extension poles. Clyde left his easel and came over. "I'm almost finished but I thought I should do something to help."

Tom gave him a thumbs up. "Thanks, Clyde, you can fill their paint troughs and if you're able, use the hand brush on the door frame."

"But the frame should be white, shouldn't it, Mister Scott? It's white in my picture."

"Oh, it will be. This is just a primer coat."

Tom walked behind Andrew and Sonny. "You two need to work as a team. When one is dipping for paint, the other should be applying. Holler for Clyde to move the trough and fill it each time you move. Glen's on the other side working alone for now."

Andrew quipped, "So, Dad, you're just going to supervise from now on?"

"Yeah, I'll be on the porch, lounging with pink lemonade." He chuckled. "No, I'm going into town for paint, gasoline and tools, but Nevaeh will be out soon with drinks and you can all take a break."

An hour later Tom pulled up to the house and saw a pushing-shouting match going on between Sonny and Andrew. Nevaeh was running to the house. Tom sprinted toward the boys. "This your idea of *teamwork*?"

Andrew pointed at Sonny. "He started it. I'll finish it."

The boys made menacing body jerks toward one another. Tom stepped between them. "Okay, that's enough." He extended his arms to separate them. "Discussion time. Let the other speak. Andrew, you first. Started what?"

The boys began to try and stare each other down adding flash grimaces for effect. Andrew spit on the ground to one side. "Called me a rich, sissy boy. I'll make that lying mouth a bloody-_"

"Stop it. Quiet now. Sonny?"

"Lazy boy quit after the juice break. He said we didn't have to work until you came back. I just told him what I thought of that."

Tom turned to his son. "True?"

Andrew shrugged.

Tom faced Sonny. "My son is not a sissy, and he sure ain't rich. However, he does have a fat lazy streak and a mean temper." Turning to Andrew, "So I think you get it. Maybe he was tackless and jellyroll, but Sonny wasn't really wrong, huh?"

His head swiveled from one to the other. "Now maybe you could each acknowledge your faults and forgive, huh?"

Reluctant "yeahs" came from each. "Good. Now I notice that Glen and Clyde have finished their side of the front. They're done for the day. You two prize fighters should have your side finished in a half hour if you work as a *team*, then we'll all have lunch."

Tom watched them as they got back to work. "If you guys are anxious to get that jeep running, you'll be glad to hear I brought back gasoline. There are some of grandpa's old tools on the bench inside, but I splurged on a basic auto tool set while I was in town."

That evening the kids were excited to describe their afternoon free time adventures. Hattie and Nevaeh described a group of ducklings swimming after their mother in a little pond nearby and being scared of a creature they saw by the woods. Tom figured they had seen a groundhog.

Clyde and Glen went over to the lake, of course, and borrowed the canoes. When they paddled close to the shore they noticed two girls in shorts on the lawn playing croquet and waving at them. Shortly, the watercraft was being shared with a boy and girl piloting each canoe. There were races, boat rammings and lots of laughter.

Andrew and Sonny had to work together, but they got the jeep running. They had to take out and clean the spark plugs, use the battery charger and shoot "Sure Start" in the carburetor. After a couple of hours they were taking turns at the wheel and bouncing up and down the driveway.

REPORTS

The first two rows of Pastor Will's church were filled on one side. He went to the lectern and moved it closer to them. "Thank you everyone for coming in on a Monday night. I know you all have other places you'd rather be, but sharing our 'out-of-comfort-zone' experiences with each other is important."

He looked up at the ceiling and gave a little laugh. "I think you'll discover that while I set this program up, God has taken it from here."

Will led them in a brief prayer before he began. "I'll call on six of you, but if anyone would like to share tonight, raise your hand." Three went up and he pointed at a woman in the front row. "Molly?"

A heavy set woman with short curly red hair and a green blazer went to the microphone. "Hi, I'm Molly. As you might know, our small satellite library way up on 2nd Avenue is pretty shabby and might close. As a teacher, I thought I could read some of their Christian Books in the children's story hour."

She smiled. "Ah, you say, easy and nonthreatening. Yeah, well that was until I got way into their fundraising auction and bake sale. Another Christian woman and I have been going door to door in these, shall we say, uncomfortable neighborhoods."

Molly took a deep breath, looked at the ceiling and blew it out through her cheeks. "That's when we realized the Holy Spirit had us out there for more than the library. Both of us are using our own money to buy up a bunch of McDonalds coupons. We've been laying on free food and telling anyone who'll listen where they can get the bread of heaven. Three were saved and two families came to our church last Sunday."

Molly received applause and "Praise Gods" as she returned to her seat. Will pointed to a lanky man in the third row. "Jim, I know you're shy, but tell us what you've been up to."

He wouldn't get up so Will handed him the microphone. "Uh, I'm Jimmy. I work back in the kitchen at The Landing restaurant. Thought I could help out making food twice a week where they feed the homeless..."

He stopped speaking, so Pastor Will spoke in a quiet voice. "It's okay, Jim. What else happened there?"

Jim's voice became croaky. "Well, I got to know some of them cause they gather outside after breakfast." He paused. "They all need help real bad. One guy is a recovering alcoholic but used to work as a chef like me. I got him cleaned up, bought him a suit so he could interview for a job and told him how Jesus changed my life."

Jim looked like he might cry but he went on. "Names' Mike. You might a seen him at church on Sunday, too. Well, he got a job now and he's sharing an apartment room not far from here." Jim was embarrassed by the applause.

He was followed by a young woman working in the local food pantry and her witness to another woman. Then there were three men: one Black, one Korean and the other, Irish. One had a guitar, another a flute and told how they wandered gangland streets together stopping to play spontaneous worship music. The trio gave their story of hope and good news to any who would listen. They got cheers with the applause.

Pastor Will pointed at him. "Okay, Ray, your turn."

"Oh shucks," Ray mumbled under his breath, but he went up to the lectern.

"Hey, look, you guys have done some wonderful things and I admire you. For me, the only uncomfortable thing was being in the sketchy neighborhood I visited, but I'm used to that now. I spend time with a hospice patient, and she knows a lot more about the Lord than I do,"

Ray looked at Will's even stare. "Obviously, I'm no great evangelist saving souls out there like some of you, but I changed my mind about quitting. I'll even talk about God if I get the chance." Will smiled.

He turned to leave, but Will stopped him. "Tell them about the other things: the boys, for example."

"Oh, yeah, well I met these two black boys outside the apartment I go to. I got to know them, shot some hoops and took them to my firehouse. No big deal, but they met Tom Scott there, a black man who befriended them. He's the real hero in this story. One boy was shot in a gang attack and then their grandmother died. Oh, and their little sister lost her best friend in the attack, too."

"Wish Tom were here. He's the one doing God's work. He invited the kids to the firehouse picnic and right now they are upstate with his whole family on some kind of work-vacation."

Ray waved down the applause. "That's for Tom. I'll tell him when he gets back."

He started to leave the podium again but Will said to the audience; "There's one more encounter, right, Ray?"

"What?" He scowled at the pastor. "I'm *not* telling them about my affair with the prostitute."

Ray's face turned red with the raucous laughter that followed. "Wait, wait, that didn't come out right at all."

His head down and heaving with suppressed laughter, he raised one finger. "Allow me to rephrase…"

Ray cleared his throat. "Quick story: A prostitute in the apartment next to Winnie's was beaten unconscious so I took her to the hospital with the help of Winnie's grand daughter, Sophia. Gosh, folks, this poor girl wasn't even fifteen."

The group became stone quiet. He took a deep breath before going on. "My idea of a prostitute used to be some slinky older woman after conventioneers at the hotel bar. But no, these are our *children* out there, hundreds, maybe thousands and thousands of them…" His head dropped. "They're caught up by human trafficking, preyed upon and enslaved."

One woman began to pray in tongues as Ray continued. "I wasn't going to say anything about this because I think we failed to help her—failed to change her life."

"We tried, though. The girl, I won't use her name, wanted to pay us back. Sophia and I told her we'd be even if she'd come to church with us once. We thought we had a breakthrough when she got emotional at the sight of a happy family, but she ran away shortly after that."

"Oh, I should mention we met a woman who runs a residential rehab just for these victims. Her name is Suzanna and the group is called Saveher. I'll give you their website if you'd like to contribute.

"I don't know if we'll ever see the girl again, but Sophia did meet her one other time. She split again before Suzanna could come and talk to her."

Ray raised his hands. "So, there it is. Sorry I couldn't give you any glowing report of salvation."

Pastor Will hastened over and stood beside him, his arm over his shoulder. "Stay a moment, Ray." He looked over the group. "He'll be shocked to hear I'm really glad you heard all this. More about that in a moment, but first I want to say how proud I am of every one of you. I wasn't sure a single soul would sign up for my 'out-of-comfort' program, but here you are on the wings of the Holy Spirit. God bless you."

Pastor Will smiled at the gathering. "Pick up your bibles and turn to James 2:26." He flipped his open on the podium. "As the body without the spirit is dead, so faith without deeds is dead."

"Many people come up with ideas of their own, deeds they think will please God or, worse yet, look good to others. The real blessing comes when we work to sense *His* presence and follow His will. This path may look messy to us sometimes but if you trust in Him, the miraculous can follow."

"Ray is a prime example. He doesn't think seeing Winnie is doing the Lord's work because she is already saved." Will slipped his arm off Ray's shoulder and grinned at him. "But you're making her last days of life useful and interesting, and just maybe the Lord is letting her help *you*."

Will turned back to the group. "Ray doesn't see how he is helping those children because his friend is doing all the interaction with them now." He chuckled. "Ray, what's the chance your friend would have ever met those kids without you?

"Lastly, this victim of human trafficking: even if you never see her again I know you've planted a flame in her heart, and besides you have put an ache in *our* hearts to help all of them. Here's the big point in all of your stories. This isn't a program your pastor controls. The Lord has taken each of you and used you for His Kingdom purpose. Remember, His plans are always better than man's plans.

"You ask, what can you do when your situation seems out of your control? Remember it's never out of His control. Search for His guidance and pray. And, speaking of that, before we go, let's bow our heads and pray right now."

FREE TIME DECISIONS

By day four, the barn had returned to the natural red color it once knew, and the jeep was waxed and polished. Andrew noticed that his dad was working in the basement, so he drove it into town, allegedly to get a garden trowel and oil for hinges, but really so he and Sonny could cruise around in the cool and the roofless.

The gray haired owner of the hardware store was fixing his door latch when they drove up. Curious about the new guys in town who sped to a dusty stop, he strolled over to their jeep. "Hey, you two, I couldn't help notice that ride of yours. Looks just like the one Wesley Scott used to ride in on, just a lot shinier. You wouldn't be a friend of his, by any chance?"

Andrew grinned. "Sure. I'm Andy Scott. He was my grandfather and he left this jeep to my dad."

The shopkeeper put out his hand. "Well, hi. I'm an Andy, too. Tell your Dad to stop in, huh? I've known him since he was half your age."

After the handshake Andy pointed his thumb at Sonny. "My friend, Sonny."

"Welcome, boys. Anything I can do for yuh?"

"Mom needs a trowel and we're out of lubricating oil."

Shopkeeper Andy pointed to their locations. "You folks movin' in, by any chance?"

"Nah, dad's going to sell Grandpa's place. You could call us if you know anyone interested in buying."

"Will do. Sorry to hear you're not staying."

"We'll be here for a few more days anyway. Know anything fun to do around here? Any theaters?"

Shopkeeper Andy laughed. "Well, not too much, unless you like hiking the Appalachian Trail or fishing. Nearest movie house is in Port Jervis, but our 'big city' is Middletown. They got a six screener."

Andy had a pained smile. "We're used to a bigger 'big city,' but we'll check it out anyway."

The man leaned to one side, looking out the front door. "Uh, you're not taking your jeep that far, are you?"

"Sure, we got it running fine, now."

"Our Sherriff's deep into a mystery novel over at the café right now. I'd suggest you scoot back home before he comes out 'cause your plates expired two years ago."

Back at the farm, Hattie screamed for Nevaeh to come quick. She dashed over from the pond to find her pointing at something in the bushes near the tree line. "Nevi, did you *ever* see anything like that?"

Nevaeh stood behind her, holding her shoulders and peering down her arm. A four foot spider web stretched between two bushes, and a very large yellow and black spider sat motionless in the middle. "Eeew," she said. "It's as big as my hand."

Hattie's eyes took a mischievous glint. "And its," A quick poke in the ribs. "Gonna getcha!"

Both ran screaming and laughing back to the house, Nevaeh reaching for a return swat.

Meanwhile, on the other side of the hill, Glen and Clyde were playing doubles badminton with Emma and Elvia. After the game, the losing team had to serve the other two on the girl's porch, but all enjoyed Emma's homemade brownies and Elvias' lemonade. For their part, the boys worked hard on impressing the girls with wildly exaggerated stories of their exploits.

Glen shamelessly lied about helping his dad put out fires in New York, but at least Clyde was right about being shot. The part about taking the bullet for someone else? Hmm, not really. Anyway, the undeserving heroes got invited for a picnic the next day at a place the girls knew on the other side of the lake.

After dinner and cleanup that evening, Tom gathered them all in the living room and scolded Andrew for taking the jeep into town. The children thought he would say something about what he and Mona had been doing during the day. Instead, Tom dropped a bombshell.

"I hate to say this, but I must. One of you stole some money from my wallet." He pointed to an empty vase on an end table. "I'll expect the money to appear in that vase sometime in the next twenty-four hours. No questions asked if it does, but if not, there will be consequences for everyone."

SONNY

Train a child in the way he should go, and
When he is old he will not turn from it. **Pr 22:6**

Late in the evening, Tom and Mona were sitting up in bed, snuggling and talking when there was a gentle rap on their door. Sonny stood there, silent and red-eyed. Tom ushered him in. "Come on in, Sonny. We're decent."

"I won't stay, I…" He thrust a wad of cash into Tom's hand. "Here. I'm the one who took it. Sorry."

Sonny turned to go but Tom restrained him. "Stay a minute. Let's talk."

"Yeah? You gonna whop me?"

Tom grasped both his shoulders and made eye contact. "Coming here was the hard way. I left an easy way for you, you know."

"Dropping it in the jar was chicken shit. I ain't no chicken."

"We have another name for your choice, Sonny. We call it honorable." He dropped his arms. "I'm proud of you, and just so you know, you're forgiven."

"Yeah—won't happen again."

"I believe you, but what if the Creeds ask you."

Sonny's glance darted around the room. "I—told you. You don't have to worry."

Tom guided him to a bedside chair. "Sit, please." He squatted down to face Sonny at eye level. "I'm worried you might still want to join that gang."

Sonny's gaze dropped to the floor and he nodded. "Now you're sounding like Grandma Helen."

"I'm sounding like the many people who care about you, Sonny."

Mona had joined them. She put her hand on Sonny's shoulder and lightly kissed the top of his head. "And I'm one of them."

Sonny's voice became croaky. "You're good folks. I knew stealing wasn't right but we always took chances when we saw them." A sole tear began to trickle down his cheek. "I thought I had blown it between us."

Mona gave his shoulder a squeeze and released it. "It would take a lot more than that, Sonny. Hey, I just realized I'm starved. Let's sneak out into the kitchen and have a little sliver of Hattie's cherry pie. What do you say?"

Shortly the three of them sat around the kitchen table sharing pie and milk. Tom said, "I think you know that stealing is wrong and a sin. All of us sin, but repentance means a change of heart and that leads to forgiveness. I hope you *also* know it's even wrong to steal from people you don't like, huh?"

Sonny was picking at his pie and spoke to his fork. "Yeah, I guess so."

"You guess so?"

"No," he looked up. "I *know* so, Mister Scott."

"Good, but we still have to discuss punishment."

"Oww," Mona cried. "Isn't that enough, Honey?"

"Nope. He's gotta show he means it."

Sonny looked as though he knew the beating would begin, but Tom said, "I understand you're taking auto mechanic training, and you did a good job on the jeep."

"Uh, yeah."

"You do such good work, I think your payback will be getting that tractor to run without pay. How about we look at it tomorrow and see what parts it needs, okay?"

Sonny sat up, his eyes glistening with excitement. "I already know. It needs a new battery and a fan belt, and I don't think anyone ever changed the differential oil."

Tom laughed. "So, you already checked it out, did you? Okay, tomorrow we'll make a list of things we need, and I'll drive over to Warwick in New York and pick them up while you guys finish painting."

"You wait and see, Mister Scott. I'll have that monster running in no time. Your grandpa left some tools and hydraulic fluid so I think I can get the road grader working too."

Tom lowered his brows. "Okay, but don't you dare try and grade the driveway all by yourself. I'm going to do that with you."

Sonny grinned and nodded enthusiastically. Mona wiggled a finger between her husband's ribs: her sign meaning "nice work, Dad."

BE READY

Suzanna and her organization were giving a presentation one evening at Ray's church. He had convinced Sophia to join him, hoping he could parlay that into a date, but she remained resistant to anything romantic.

Suzanna spoke from the podium. "While all these girls are victims, most don't realize they are actually being used as slaves for profit. Desperate to find anything resembling family, they cling to their handlers as the only life structure they know. They are captured by not knowing any other way to support themselves and usually by drug addiction as well. Sadly, there are well over a million such girls in the U.S. and after they're captured they have an average lifespan of seven years.

"Your handout reviews how you can spot these victims and the agencies to whom you can report them. Rarely will a parent be the rescuer since they frequently run away from any home they see as threatening. Usually police or other governmental agencies are needed to get them stabilized initially.

"They may place these girls in foster care, shelters, or group homes, but they cannot be locked up in juvenile hall without a conviction, so usually they end up running away and returning to their pimps. We try our best to get as many girls into our Christian residential center as possible. Currently, our Saveher Ranch is caring for seven residents, and running away is rare." Sophia had her hand up. "Yes?"

"Why is your facility any different from the others you mentioned? The one victim I had contact with is pretty leery about Christianity."

"Good point, Sophia. They usually don't try to run away from our ranch because the nearest building through the woods is six miles away. We watch monitors to make sure would-be escapees don't hurt themselves."

"The girls may stay with us from months to years. We give them health care and complete their education and skill training. In my opinion, the most important thing we do for our girls is to let them discover they have a loving father in Heaven. Only when our girls are comfortable with God's presence, are they ready to take on the challenges of our world with confidence. For if He is with us, who can stand against us?"

Ray's cell phone sounded, and Suzanna asked everyone to silence theirs. "We will now be breaking up into four discussion groups with the Saveher staff here to…"

Ray rushed up to her with the message from Winnie. "Ray, come right away. Rachel is here on my couch."

Suzanna took the microphone. "Change of plans, folks: *three* groups. I have to leave on an emergency."

THE LAST DAY

The house and barn never looked better, and everyone was impressed with Clyde's watercolor. No doubt it would look great in the "for sale" ads. Mona set her camera on a fence post for a timer shot of everyone. That required four takes and a warning shout from Tom, thanks to the kids horsing around before each camera click.

All the youngsters had different ideas on what to do on their last day on the farm. Hattie had mixed up an enormous bowl of cookie dough to prepare for today and the trip back to New York. Some wanted more fishing on the lake, some wanted to go on the hiking trails in the hills and still others thought that video games, lounging around and finishing Hattie's cookies would be just fine. For the morning, would be none of the above.

It was Sunday and Tom and Mona were determined to take everyone to grandpa's old church across the line in New York State. The groans and moans sounded like a pack of wounded coyotes, but the grown ups did their best to get everyone looking decent and packed into their van.

Grandpa's little white, wooden church nestled into green farm fields, and was remarkably like the classic post cards. Glen grabbed Clyde by the shirt and whispered. "Don't stare, but check out who's coming in from the parking lot."

Their eyes bugged out anyway. The girls, Elvia and Emma, dressed in elegant print dresses, were walking with their grandpa, and apparently their parents. The two families met in front of the church and introduced themselves. The girl's mother picked out Clyde and Glen right away. "Hello, I'm Louise. You boys must be the ones our girls keep talking about."

Emma poked at her, whispering, "Ma-uh-m." She and her sister went about silent glancing and smiling with the boys.

Everyone enjoyed the heartfelt worship and preaching in the service despite the fidgeting of the junior high set. Afterward, Louise spoke for her family. "Look, we came to pick up our daughters but we're not leaving for home until tomorrow. We'd planned a picnic this afternoon, and we'd love to have you come. It's just that we don't have that much food."

"You mean you think the eight of us including four boys might eat a little?" Mona laughed. "This week's been like feeding a herd of cattle for us but, don't worry. We stocked up with food for our return trip. Our little Hattie here made enough cookies for the Marines. We'll be there in about two hours."

Hattie really loved the "our" in what Mona said, and gave her a long hug.

146

THE SAVIORS

Suzanna told Ray and Sophia to go straight to Winnie's and detain Rachel. She'd be there soon. When they arrived, Rachel lay on her side with her shirt pulled up, exposing a purple bruise. Winnie's wheelchair was alongside the couch. She was rubbing Rachel's hands and singing to her.

Ray knelt on the floor beside them. "Hey, girl. We gotta stop meeting like this."

He got a half smile, but it was Winnie who spoke. "She says it hurts to take a deep breath and talk. That so called boyfriend of hers *kicked* her."

Rachel spoke in a loud whisper. "That fn___ bas___! Claims I'm two Franklins short. Maybe he could a got the John to put it in writing, huh? Now he expects me to go out and walk the strip 'til I earn it back."

Winnie began to massage her shoulder. "You don't have to go anywhere, my dear. You can stay here as long as you like."

Rachel bestowed a genuine smile and spoke in a whisper. "You're one hell of a nice lady, Winnie. Sorry to bother you, but I couldn't think of any other safe place."

Ray had been poking around the bruise while they talked. "I don't think the rib is broken, but I'm going to strap you up anyway. We call this an intercostal sprain. The tape will limit your deep breaths and prevent painful movement."

She opened her eyes wide. "Darn! So you're *not* giving me a big shot of morphine?"

He scowled, and she started to chuckle but winced. Ray grinned. "I know you're kidding. Best I can do is two Advils."

"I'm trying to cut back on the hard stuff, honest. It's not easy."

Sophie came closer. "I'm proud of you for trying, but it would be a lot easier if you let Jesus do the hard work for you."

Rachel rolled her eyes, then looked at Sophia. "Hey, you two are always together. You boinking, huh?"

Sophie snorted but Ray answered. "We're not into premarital boinking, kid. Now raise your arms up so I can get the tape around."

Ray made several circles of her torso with tape. She scrunched her nose. "You making me into a mummy or what? That's gonna hurt coming off."

"First layer is paper tape, so that won't be…"

The doorbell rang and Sophie hurried to answer it. Suzanna entered with a big smile but Rachel scowled. "Sh---, who told *her* I was here?"

Suzanna walked toward her speaking softly. "I hope we can just talk a bit."

Rachel made it to a sitting position wincing as she went. "Just talk, huh? I told you. I ain't gonna go to your funny farm, sister."

"No one will force anything on you, Rachel, but we have half a dozen girls there, and some are old acquaintances of yours."

Rachel scowled at Sophia. "You called her on me, didn't you?"

"Oh, Rachel, just listen to what she has to say. She only means to help."

Suzanna squatted down to face her on eye level. "Not only will you get good medical care and education, but we can get your parole violation removed."

Rachel was almost shouting. "You *know* about that?"

"Yes, and it can go away. Otherwise you'll spend one to two years in jail for both the crime and the violation."

She struggled to stand up with a grunt. "Okay, this is getting weird." Bursting through them, she headed for the door. "I've had it with all of you. I'm f---g out of here."

Two female officers stood in the hall outside and grabbed her as the door opened. They deftly handcuffed her through screams and profanity.

Suzanna rushed over to stand in front of them. She ignored a spit in her face. "Rachel, dear, this was going to happen one day anyway. I promise you: tonight will be your only day behind bars if you choose a new life with us. I'll be with you and your appointed lawyer at your hearing tomorrow."

She stared back in silent anger. Suzanna continued. "We do this because we really care about you, Rachel. By tomorrow, heaven will have heard a hundred prayers for you, some of them from girls you know. We're praying you'll choose life. God bless you."

The officers turned her around to leave. Winnie called through the open door. "You be sure and write me now."

CHANGE OF PLAN

The American Museum of Natural History is huge. Summer was almost over, and The Scotts were taking their favorite "street kids" on another excursion. Tom and Mona chose the formal tour with the boys except for Andrew who had taken up a conversation with some girl and waved everyone away with hand signals behind his back. Nevaeh and Hattie were off doing their own "tour". They had mother's cell phone and strict orders to call in regularly.

Nevaeh was supposed to call Dad's phone every ten minutes per plan, but once they just waved at them from a balcony instead, and charged down the corridor in a hail of giggles. In the last call, mother was informed that Hattie had been eaten by a Velociraptor. How sad.

Clyde saw that everyone else was busy and he drew close to Mona looking up at her with a new intensity of expression. He spoke in a loud whisper. "Uh, Missus Scott, can I ask you something in private? It's important."

"Why, of course, Dear. Let's go over here."

151

They sat on a stone bench, the skeleton of a mastodon looking on behind them. "Uh, we have a plan. Sonny and I have things figured out—uh, mostly. He'll finish high school in less than a year and get a job in mechanics. I'll live with him and finish too. See, we ain't gonna join no gang."

"Hey, I like that." Mona smiled. "It might be even easier if they find a foster home for you, and maybe we can help Sonny find employment."

Clyde grimaced. "Yeah, well I can tell there's not going to be a foster home for all of us. Me and Sonny are worried about Hattie. We don't want to leave her by herself, but we can't take care of her either."

"Oh, Clyde," She tapped her chest. "It's wonderful you care about your sister's welfare, but if anyone can be placed in a good home it would be spunky little Hattie."

"Yeah, that's right. Here's the thing. We hope you guys would take her in. Could you?"

"Well," Mona sat upright. "That's a big decision, and we already have three children."

"I know, but just think about it, huh? Look at how she is with Nevaeh."

Mona stood up and he did also. She grasped his shoulders and spoke with furrowed brow. "Don't get your hopes up for that, Clyde. However, I will speak to Tom about it. Either way, I know Hattie will be all right."

Clyde grinned, his face filled with radiant hopefulness. "Okay, Missus Scott."

When they returned to the others, Tom asked his wife, "Where'd you two go? Do you suppose your Dora the Explorer could take a break and join us for lunch in the cafeteria? Andrew's a lost cause, but I'll call him anyway."

Mona dialed the girls' number. "You guys are late for your call in.--Uh, huh, why there?—Uh huh—Well, all right."

She faced her family. "Nevaeh wants to meet us up on the third floor where the dioramas are. She says it's important. We're supposed to see them at the Ice Age display."

Glen said, "I don't suppose she said why. I'm hungry."

Mona smiled. "You know your sister. She just said it was important."

The dioramas were life-sized replicas of life in ages past, artfully creating the feeling of actually being there. No sign of "Dora." Dad's phone rang. "I can see you, Dad." Giggles, "Come up closer."

Tom spun around. "Nevaeh, we don't have time for hide and seek."

"We're not hiding." More giggles. "We're *watching* you. Come up to the glass and look in."

Dad took his wife's hand. "Uh oh, Mona."

They stood looking into the diorama. Off to one side was a primitive human family gathered around a fire in front of a huge glacier. On the other side a saber-toothed tiger stalked a wooly mammoth. Tom did a 360, thinking their pranksters had snuck up behind them. "Okay, you two," he spoke into his phone. "No more games."

"No game, Dad. You're too tall. Squat down and look between the mammoth legs."

Mona had her ear near the phone. They exchanged worried looks and bent down to look. There in the open workmen's hatch two little black faces grinned back at them, hands waving. Mother said, "Aach."

Daddy said, "Get back out here right away. You want to be arrested?"

The boys said, "Ha ha ha ha."

Nevaeh assumed her adult voice, and flashed badges dangling from their necks. "It's quite all right, Father. We are guests of Doctor Ekland. He's one of the anthropologists here."

"My God. And you met him where?"

"In the elevator. You always said not to be afraid to ask questions of responsible grown ups."

"Okay, I'm impressed, Nevaeh, but unless you're on a lecture tour, do you suppose you could meet us in the cafeteria and do some explaining?"

She stood up and turned away. "Sure, Dad. Got to turn in the badges first." Hattie gave a happy wave and closed the hatch.

Andrew was a no show in the cafeteria and, he was not answering his phone. When they were seated, his text came in: "Having lunch across the street. Catch you this afternoon."

Mona looked at the text. "Our boy's growing up, and unfortunately Tom, he has your good looks."

While munching sandwiches, Nevaeh told Dad how she could tell Doctor Ekland was a professor so she started asking him lots of questions about the Aztecs. Impressed, he invited them to the fifth floor work area. After an Aztec lecture, he turned them over to Martha Walsh, a graduate student. She gave them badges, a personal tour of the scientists work area and a hug.

Nevaeh said, "She's really nice. She gave me her phone number and said if my parents okayed it, I could come back anytime."

Mona pointed her finger at her. "But I'll bet she *also* said you were to phone your parents and tell us where you were, right?"

"Well, I did—kinda."

"Sure, that's when you said you were just looking at Mayan pottery, huh?"

Tom chuckled. "Alright, no harm done. Look, I wanted to talk to all of you about something more serious. Andrew knows about this already."

Mona rested her face on her hand and searched the children's faces. "Some of you might be upset about this but I want you to know this won't change anything between us."

Tom cleared his throat. "Um, Andrew didn't get his scholarship and his student loan is a small one, but he's starting college in a few weeks. This is going to be a financial burden on us and we've decided to sell our condo and move to a less expensive place nearby."

Sonny sat up abruptly. "How far away, Mister Scott?"

"We don't know yet, but hopefully, not so far we still can't get together once in awhile."

Clyde scrunched his face. "Once in awhile?"

Mona put her hand on Hattie's who was hunched over and looked like she was on the verge of tears. "Maybe there won't be weekend play dates every week, but we're *not* forgetting you guys."

Nevaeh hugged Hattie. "Me neither. There's *nothing* gonna keep us apart."

Tom went on. "I've applied for jobs in Newark and Peekskill. We shouldn't be more than an hour from Manhattan."

Clyde and Sonny stared at the floor in sullen silence. Hattie was sitting up and taking a bite of dessert. "Hattie," Mona said. "I meant to tell you how much I appreciated that thank you card you sent us. You look like want to say something."

Hattie poked at her plate. "They put too much sugar in the lemon pie. Don't they know *anything*? It's supposed to be more tart."

FARAWAY THOUGHTS

Winnie had become bedridden and Sophie moved into her spare bedroom so she wouldn't be alone at night. She sat on the edge of her grandmother's bed and brought her face close to Winnie's when she stirred. "Ah, grandma, there. I thought you were awake. Can I make you more comfortable or get you something to drink?"

Winnie wheezed with each breath but she managed a thin smile. "A little ice water would be nice."

"You got it, Nana." Sophie cranked up the head of the hospital-type bed. "Be right back."

She returned with the glass, cubes clinking and a lemon slice poking up on one side. "Here you go."

Winnie softly croaked "thank you," and cleared her throat. "Leave the bed up like this. I can breathe better."

"Absolutely. And while you were sleeping, the mail came. You have to guess who sent you a letter."

"My deceased husband saying hurry up already."

Sophie stuck her tongue out at her. "Oh, you. You're even funny when you're being morbid. Guess again."

"Increased property taxes, maybe?"

"No, silly, it's from Rachel, and I didn't want to open it until you woke up."

"Now, that is a surprise—not as big as one from my *son* would be, but a surprise."

She tapped the pillow behind her. "Could you crank this thing up one more notch first?"

Sophie cranked and opened. "Here we go."

"*Dear Winnie,*

Hope you are well. Starting my fourth week here at prison camp. I'll be fair. It's better than jail but this place is full of Jesus freaks."

Sophie paused while they chuckled. She fanned herself with the letter. "She knew that going in, Grandma."

"Sure, but God seems like foolishness to those who are perishing, doesn't He? Read on."

"The first week was the worst, Winnie. I always thought I could give up the happy pills anytime I wanted to. I'm not shaking anymore, but man, I still want one. I still feel I want to go back to my 'boyfriend,' the boss. Funny, huh?

"On the good side, Saveher Ranch food is pretty good and I met an old friend of mine here. Name's Natasha. We used to bunk together, and here we are again. Lots of old stories.

"Hey, here's a weird one. I can't get that little girl, Kali, out of my head. Something happened inside of me when she did

160

that prayer thing. Ask Sophie to give her a hug for me and tell her I'm okay, huh?"

Sophie covered her mouth and blinked her eyes as emotion came over her. She let out a breath and continued.

"Gotta get some sleep now. The slave drivers get us up early and I'm supposed to hoe out weeds in the corn patch tomorrow. You stay well.

Rachel"

Winnie croaked softly. "Take down a response for me?"

Sophie found a pad and pulled up a chair. "Shoot, Nana."

"Dearest Rachel, just know we all love you. I wish I could visit because I won't be here when you come back to New York."

Sophie put her hand on Winnie's arm. "Don't say that, Grandma. You don't really know that."

Winnie tapped Sophie's hand and continued. "The really exciting thing is that you are about to make the greatest, most joyful discovery of your life. You don't believe me now, but I foresee that you will soon realize you're loved and valued by God. You are about to know you are forgiven and your past will be left behind. I only wish I could be there when that happens. Sophie will give you a big squeeze for me next time you see her."

Sophie grinned. "That's really sweet, Granny, and prophetic, too. Anything else?"

Winnie took a few wheezing breaths and smiled back. "I don't think so. Sign it 'Love, Grandma Winnie,' okay?"

FLOATING DECISION

Your Father in heaven is not willing that any
Of these little ones should be lost. MT 18: 14

The Liberty Island day cruiser roared its diesel engines and moved out and down the Hudson River, the huge buildings of the Financial Center on the left and smaller ones in Newark on the right. Sonny, Clyde and Hattie clung to the railing watching the concrete dock grow smaller.

Mona put her hand on Hattie's shoulder. Her round, expectant face looked up at her. She asked, "When are we going to meet up with Nevie and the others?"

"In twenty minutes or so, but not Andrew. He's at a college orientation. Your school starts in a week, but they begin early. Our children will get on at another stop. They're with Ray and Sophie."

Tom came over to them. His voice was low and purpose-filled. "I want all of you come up to the prow. We have something really important to talk about."

Mona gathered them on a bench seat along the railing, her arms around Hattie and Clyde while Tom stood in front of them

163

clearing his throat. "My first announcement is about my new job. My friend Mike at our firehouse came up with the job opportunity, and I don't know why I didn't think of it myself. Can you guess where I'll be working soon?"

Sonny pouted. "Los Angeles, right?"

Tom chuckled. "Mike found this on the Internet. Sullivan County in New York is undergoing a transition. They were looking for a Fire Chief from outside their area and they hired me at my first interview. Can you believe it?"

Clyde asked, "Is it farther than Peekskill?"

"Yes, but a lot closer than Los Angeles." He grinned at Sonny. "Our problem seemed to be we couldn't sell the farm despite Clyde's truly righteous watercolor."

Mona gave the kids a little squeeze. "That's when we started praying. I have to keep learning this myself. Remember, kids, don't try important things without God's help."

"With prayer, things began to happen." Tom raised his hands. First, Andrew did get a small scholarship, and then we got a hugely generous offer on our Manhattan condo. Bottom line is, we're moving into the farm house."

Hattie straightened up and turned her big, pleading eyes toward Mona. "Can we come and spend summer vacation with you? Please, please."

Mona gave her a quick forehead kiss and pointed at Tom. "Of course, but there's more. Listen."

164

Tom cleared his throat again. "Now, here's the *big* question for all three of you." He squatted down to be at their eye level just as the boat went through a wake.

"Whoa." He regained his balance and tried kneeling. "Half this decision was ours. The other half will be yours. We made sure the papers would be okay and we all voted as a family. It was a unanimous yes, four and a half to nothing. There was one 'maybe, I guess' but that's half a yes. Now you have to vote. Take your time. You can do it in private if you want."

The children sat quietly for a moment. Sonny raised his hand. "Uh, Mister Scott?"

"Yes, Sonny?" He glanced at his wife who was suppressing a laugh.

"You didn't say what we are voting on. Are you gonna foster one of us? "

Tom raised one finger and made a funny face. "Oops, I didn't explain, did I? We all want all of you to become part of our family, that is, we want to *adopt* you."

Mona beheld three wide-eyed, open-mouth faces. "That means we love you and Tom and I want so very much to be your forever Mom and Dad."

Hattie exploded up from the bench with a shriek and began jumping up and down. Clyde was next, pulling Mona to her feet. The four of them embraced as Hattie still tried to jump saying, "Yes, yes, oh *yes*."

Sonny rose slowly and stood at a distance eyeing Tom with a furrowed brow. "You want me, too?"

Tom extended his arm. "You, most of all. Come here, son."

Sonny fell into the group hug, tears beginning to come. "We all talked about this—hoped it could happen—but never thought it *would* happen."

Mona had tears of her own. "I guess this means you're voting yes. We just love all of you. This all seems so right."

Sonny said, "And I'm gonna be better. You'll see."

Tom hugged him around the shoulders. "Of course you will. Besides, who could we count on to keep our jeep and tractor running?"

The boat nosed down and began angling toward its first stop. Nevaeh could be seen jumping up and down from a half mile out.

Mona chuckled. "As you can see, we knew our kids couldn't keep this a secret."

Nevaeh was the first on board, Sophie trying to keep her from falling overboard off the ramp. She and Hattie embraced and began a happy, spinning dance, singing. "Sisters, sisters, we're gonna be sisters."

Glen came up to Clyde and Sonny and fist bumped. "Hey, welcome to the family, guys."

Mona gave Sophie and Ray a quick embrace. "So sorry to leave you with them, but we knew this was going to be a hard secret to keep even though we confiscated Glen's cell phone."

Ray laughed. "But Nevaeh was pretty resourceful. She borrowed mine with the excuse of calling you, but I caught her using a matronly voice talking to reception at the juvenile home. Obviously she was about to spill the beans." He looked around. "Where'd they go?"

"Hattie had the Shuffleboard Court staked out. They might be playing Hopscotch on it."

Sonny stuck close to Tom, but Glen and Clyde were having a serious discussion on the other side of the boat. Glen spoke as he looked toward the Jersey shore. "You know, those girls only come to the lake for occasional vacations."

"Yeah, but they go to school nearby. Too bad we'll live in New Jersey. That's another school district."

"Wait a sec, Clyde. Dad said County employees can send their kids to school near where they work if they want to."

"Cool. And, Glen, the tall one *really* likes you. I can tell."

"Elvia? Maybe but Emma got all mushy when you said you'd been shot."

Clyde nodded. "She worries a lot, that one. But she did like my drawings."

Glen gave him a fist tap on the shoulder. "So, you were working all the angles, huh? And I just remembered. What was

167

Emma doing looking under your collar? You showed her your scar, didn't you?"

He laughed. "Well, she asked. By the way, I made sketches of everyone, the girls too. They're back in my room."

Glen grinned. "Really? Portraits of the girls? Oh man, they'll melt before our eyes. I see double dates coming up fast. If only we were old enough to drive."

PROMISE

Hattie and Nevaeh were standing on tiptoe looking out of Lady Liberty's crown. They waved at the ships coming their way even though no one on board could see them. Hattie ran over to the view port on Liberty's far left and looked back at the skyscrapers on the tip of Manhattan. "Nevi, have you ever lived outside the city before?"

"Uh, uh. That week on the farm was my first."

"We're gonna have to get used to living with all them bugs and mice, and you're scared of the mice."

"You are *too*, Hattie. Remember the mouse you saw in the kitchen?"

"Yeah, but you beat me out the door."

Nevaeh laughed. "I was more scared of your scream than the mouse."

"All right, so we're even, but I have a plan to get them out of my kitchen."

"So, ten minutes after you're adopted, it's become *your* kitchen?"

She giggled. "Aw, you know what I mean." Hattie rolled her eyes. "But if we work together, maybe we can convince Mona, er, mother, to let us have a cat."

"Whoa," Nevaeh grinned. "Genius. She wouldn't let me have one in the city, but what's a farm house without a cat? And I have an idea too. Mice have germs. Mom *hates* germs."

"Perfect. Before we ask, we just keep talkin' about mice and germs. Bet we'll get a kitty real soon." They did a fist bump.

The alarm went off on the cell phone they'd been given. "Time to get back on the boat." Nevaeh began to edge toward the stairwell. She glanced down at the long and winding descent. "Race you downstairs."

When everyone had returned to the day cruiser, Tom and Mona summoned the kids back to the prow for their first family meeting. The wind had picked up, and the boat was splashing through the wakes of cargo ships. Tom stood at the prow and faced them. "So, everyone, how do you like the Scott Family Boardroom?"

Mona sat next to him, her hand up around his waist. "We thought we'd say a few words to you kids while your all together. We're about to be going to be through a lot of changes in all our lives."

"Beside the obvious, we mean." Tom nodded. "I will be starting a new, very responsible job, and we're not only moving but changing from city to country life."

Mona nodded, "Just know in advance that this will be stressful, and frustrating at times, but were all in this together. We want all of you kids to know we're here for you, but we hope we can count on your help, too. We want to be parents who listen and care."

Tom "pistol pointed" at Nevaeh and Glen swinging his pointer fingers up and down. "I want to say I'm proud of you two." He turned to Hattie, Sonny and Clyde. My kids are okay with full equality with you guys. No favoritism. You are the same as if you were born to us."

"That's right," Mona smiled at them. "Just like Christians adopted by the Jewish Messiah."

Tom followed a low swooping seagull with his eyes for a moment but he focused back on the children. "Frankly, the guys at the firehouse think I've lost it, but the good news is we know that the Lord is with us. There'll be work ahead, but I think I can promise we'll have a lot of fun times, too."

He pointed at Ray who was standing to one side with Sophia. "That rather modest friend of mine brought us together with a church program called 'out of your comfort zone' and we wouldn't be here without him."

Ray shrugged. "Just serendipity?"

Mona shook her head. "Nope, that was a 'God wink.' When God gives you an assignment, things that happen are no coincidence."

Sophia was grinning. "Seeing you all together like this gives me the fuzzies."

Tom gestured with his hands. "So, look, the truth is, we'll all be mixing good times with some troubles and mistakes ahead, me included. But here's my pitch as your father: I will lay down the rules, but I promise to be patient and forgiving."

Mona took her husband's hand and spread out her arms to the children. Tom grinned. "Gather in all of you, Ray and Sophie too. We're going to do a dedication."

The other passengers looked on curiously as a white couple helped form a circle with a large black family. Tom looked skyward. "Dear Lord, we, your children, are *so* happy to be gathered here in your name. We sense Your presence right now, bringing us together. Mona and I dedicate this new family to You and we stand in full expectation of Your guidance and your love."

"And I pray," Mona added, "that each of these children come into a full relationship with Jesus, our Savior. Amen."

Sonny cleared his throat. "I, uh, as the oldest of the Jacksons, want to thank you for taking us in. I just hope we don't ruin your life. I only remember a little of my mother, but none of us ever had a father." He looked at his shoes for a moment, coughed and said, "I think I can speak for all of us. We're real, *real* glad we have one now."

Ray and Sophie joined in the laughing, tearful group hug that followed. Glen stood at the prow and pointed ahead. "Here's a song these old folks used to sing." He looked at dad. "The travel song, how's it start?"

Tom smiled but only sang the first word, "Oh..."

Then everyone joined in. "Oh, we ain't got a barrel of money. Maybe we're ragged and funny, but we'll travel along, singing a song—side by side."

Tom jiggled his wife's arm. "What's the next verse?"

Mona jumped up on the seat in the prow. "Through all kinds of trouble..." A big wave splashed up and over them, and all anyone could do was laugh.

RACHEL, IS THAT YOU?

"Dear Winnie,

"Sorry if it's been awhile since I last wrote. Hope you've been well. It has been a beautiful fall out here in the sticks. My favorite color is the one that looks like rust.

"I'm into sort of a routine here and I'm back in school right here on campus. They want us to move up to our grade level so we can get through high school when we get out of here. Yeah, they don't keep us forever. One of the courses is music and I love it. Julia Martin is our teacher and she says my singing voice is special. Imagine that.

Can you believe we had a rock group give us girls a concert here? They're called 'Connecting Worlds.' You'd like them 'cause they sang about Jesus and the Father. Julia told them I could sing and they let me do one cut. Wow, that was fun.

"It's hard to talk about, Winnie, but I found out I was really a victim of people using me. I guess we girls thought our handlers were saving us from death on the streets, but we were just making money for them. I haven't been touched by a man in months now, and frankly, I don't care if I never see a man again. (No offense, Ray.)

"I thought they'd be real pushy about religion here, but it's not like that. Sure, we have church on Sunday, but the real push to Jesus is other girls like me telling their stories. When I first got here, I could tell some girls were different and Natalie was one of them. These girls are full of hope and confidence. They reach out to help you and they really care. No fake stuff.

"The main thing on my mind, Winnie, is to tell you that what you prayed for came true. Last week two girls and Suzanna led me in prayer. I accepted Jesus Christ as my Lord and Savior and God the Father is my father now. Oh, Winnie, it feels so good inside. We all had the biggest cry when I did this, and I'm crying again, just telling you.

"Oops, it's lights out. I'll write again.

"Love to you, Sophia and Ray,

"Rachel.

When she read this letter, Sophia had a good cry herself—a happy one. While they weren't seeing much of each other anymore, she wanted to share the letter with Ray, but it took a couple of days before she was ready to reply.

She read the letter and her reply to Ray on the phone. "Dear Rachel, It is with great sadness I must tell you that my grandmother passed away a few weeks ago. On her last day she told me, 'You look after Rachel when she gets out of camp. She's going to be a fine young woman one day. I just know it'."

"So, Rachel, I don't know when that will be, but if you like, you're welcome to live with me when that time comes. Ray and I are good friends but not the romantic kind.

"I don't have words to express how happy I am that you have found the Lord. I'm going to apologize to you right now for doubting it would ever happen. I think you'll find in the years ahead that the closer you get to God, the more you'll have joy and surprises.

"Guess who asks about you every time I see her? Kali. I think you are the first person she has tried to heal with prayer and she wants to know how you're doing. I asked her if she worries about you. 'Oh, yeth,' she said, so I'm glad I can give her a good report on Sunday.

"Please write again when you can.

"Love, Sophie and Ray.

FIELD REPORT

"Dear Sophia and Ray, Sorry again for not writing back sooner. I took me awhile to get used to the idea of not ever seeing Winnie again. You must miss her even more and I am sorry for you.

"Did you give Kali a hug for me? Tell her that it was her prayer that made my sadness go away. When I get back to New York, I'll give her a big squeeze myself.

"We've been really busy here. Winter must come early in the country 'cause we have a foot of snow and it's not even Christmas. We girls went out with a shovel brigade and cleaned the walks yesterday. It was such fun even if I was the snowball fight loser. Thank you for the early Christmas present of boots and a coat. I'll be using them every day.

"This is gonna sound strange, but last week I got my body back. Every day we have a Christian study session and our teacher explained that our bodies were given to us by God and His Spirit is inside us. Me and my friends were giving ours away. No more. My body is mine.

"Speaking of my body, I have been given a clean bill of health by the doctor. Many of us had chronic infections around

our inside female organs but we all got treated. Doctor said I
was lucky because I still have a good ovary and could have kids.
'Course I'm thinking that'll never happen.

"Gotta go now.

"Love, Rachel."

Sophia held the letter to her chest and sent back a prayer. She made a copy of the letter and mailed it to Ray with a note: "You did good, kid!"

Her reply: "Dear Rachel, Your letters warm my heart. I know my mother was right about you and I want to be in that hug celebrating with you and Kali.

"Here's some news. Ray treated one of your friends who was wounded in a street shooting. She will only give her name as Carmel Candy. Sound familiar? Suzanna is all over it, and we have hopes she'll join you after she transfers out of the hospital. If you want to pass her a note, I'll give it to her. Maybe she'll come to Saveher Ranch if you ask.

Oh, and here's a little whisper between us girls, a secret. A friend of mine works in hospital administration. This gal is a real matchmaker. Well, she met a newly hired nurse in her mid twenties, who started working at North General. My sneaky friend worked out an introduction to Ray they have been out twice together. Don't tell anyone, but she's crazy about him. Really bonkers. Go figure.

"Keep your snowbound letters coming. Love, Sophie"

"Dear Sophie and Ray,

"They're letting me out—well, sort of. The teachers say that three of us are ready to finish up a last semester at ninth grade. Then we can start high school in the fall. I'll be a year older than my classmates, but I don't care. We live at a juvenile shelter in Middletown during the week, and then back here for the weekend. I'm a little nervous about being in school again.

"Here's a note for Carmel. Yeah, I know her. Word of warning: she's had training as a kickboxer.

"Hey, Carmie, it's Kit. Bet you thought I was dead, huh? Well, I'm dead to that old world on the streets, sister. Glad to hear you'll recover from your wound.

"Listen, I've been at Saveher Ranch for the past few months, and I think you should come join me. Natalie's here too. I fought the idea just like you will, but trust me, this is a good way out of hell. It's worth it. Good food, your own bed and great company, like me. Ha, ha.

"Seriously, you won't regret it—except when you're going off the happy pills, but you'll come down off them holding hands with people who actually care about you, seriously. So, I'm counting on you. Get your ass over here.

"Kit

FORGIVENESS

Forgive each other just as in Christ,
God forgave you. **Eph 4: 32**

Rachel sat in an Adirondack chair, alone on a broad wooden deck, staring out at the woodsy view. She tried to calm herself. *So, I'm supposed to have a private talk with Suzanna, huh. Either I've done something wrong or she's gonna lay something big on me. I can just feel it.*

She got up, leaned out over the railing and watched the birds flitting around on the feeder. Winter wasn't over yet and a gust of wind caused her to pull up the collar on her coat. *Stop it, Rachel. Hopefully, this will be just one of those 'how's it going' meetings before I start school next week.*

Rachel turned around when the slider opened behind her. Two women with overly pleasant smiles approached her. *Oh crap, the pastor's with Suzanna.*

"Hi, Rachel," Suzanna voice was especially gentle. "This is just a friendly chat. If it's too cold out here, we can go inside."

"Nah, I'm fine." She looked pastor Sue in the eye. "Look, if this is about me swearing yesterday, I'm sorry--repentant even. It just slipped out."

Sue chuckled. "Nonsense, I didn't even know about it. Just tell God you're sorry. He knows your heart and He's full of forgiveness." She motioned to the chairs. "Let's sit."

Rachel sat, scowled and glanced from one to the other. "Just so you know, you guys are making me real nervous. This is something about school tomorrow, isn't it?"

Suzanna said, "No, we briefed all of you about that yesterday but, of course, you can ask me any questions you might have."

Sue cleared her throat and delivered a concerned, penetrating look. "We wanted to talk to you about what I just mentioned: forgiveness."

"Thought you said I was forgiven when I accepted Jesus."

"You are, my Dear. You are, and just as He forgives you, you can forgive others. It's an important part of your new Christian life and, surprisingly, one that will give you great pleasure."

"I know, and it's in the Lord's Prayer. Our instructor said we should forgive someone who doesn't deserve it, and it doesn't mean you have to *like* them or approve of what they are doing."

Suzanna perked up. "Oh, good. Maybe this'll be a short visit. Who'd you pick?"

Rachel tossed her head and pursed her lips. "Natasha and I both picked our bosses, you know, those tough guys who sometimes like to beat up on us girls. They don't deserve *nothing* good, but we asked God to forgive them all the same." She gave them a triumphant grin.

"Way to go, Rachel." Pastor Sue returned a thumbs up. "How did you feel after you did?"

She pouted. "You're right. We both felt better inside."

"See, that pent up hate hurts you, and has no effect on the other person."

Rachel leaded forward to get up, a "we're done now, right?" look on her face.

Suzanna motioned for her to sit back, leaned forward and lowered her voice. "This is a good start for where we are going today, Rachel. When you get back into that outside world your biggest challenge, in my experience, will be getting back a normal relationship with men."

"No problem," Rachel pouted. "I'll just cross the street anytime I see one coming."

"I know you're being silly, but you're making my point." Suzanna sighed and made eye contact. "I'll just get right to it. Men will always be a relationship problem until you resolve your feelings for your father."

"Holy s___!" Rachel jumped up, eyes and nostrils flaring. "If this is about forgiving *him,* forget it."

Pastor Sue stood up beside her. "Oh, my dear, we know how painful this is for you, but please just hear us out."

Rachel backed against the deck rail and gave a silent, flick of the wrist gesture with her hands.

Suzanna remained seated and waited for Rachel to look at her. "An important part of rehabilitation for you girls is researching the status of your family."

Rachel shot back, "Easy for me. Ain't got none."

"Seven years ago your parents were in financial difficulty and they were having violent arguments. The neighbors in your apartment called the police twice. Your father lost his job as a machinist when the company went bankrupt, and two other jobs didn't last long. He made the mistake of joining a gang who rob banks and ended up in prison. Do you remember how old you were at the time?"

She plunked back into her seat. "Nine or ten I think."

"You were nine. Ever visit him?"

"No, and Ma only went once. We moved to a rented room and lived on welfare and disability. Ma hit the booze like crazy and died a few years later. Never got so much as *one* letter from jail."

Pastor Sue put her arm around her shoulders. "And that left you completely alone."

Suzanna nodded. "Child protective services tried to locate you, but failed. Why did you disappear into Manhattan?"

"Emma, a friend of mine in an older grade, went there a year earlier. Thought I could live with her and get work but her number was discontinued and I never found her."

Suzanna grinned. "Not that it matters now, but it was illegal to cash your mom's disability check after she died. How old were you then?"

Rachel squirmed around in her chair. "What is this, the Spanish Inquisition? Maybe thirteen, I guess."

"No more questions, then, but here's an update. Your dad was released from prison well over a year ago. His public defender proved to the parole board that while he drove the getaway car, he had no knowledge of the gun under his seat."

"Like I care. Can I go now?"

"Patience. While in prison your father was ministered to by Kairos who led him to Christ. They also helped find him a machinist's job, and here's a coincidence: it's in Middletown where you'll be going to school."

Rachel released a sigh. "Look, I know you guys mean well, but you can't make me see him."

"Of course not, but you should know he met a woman in church, and has been married for three months now."

"You're not going to tell him where I am, are you?"

Pastor Sue put her hand on Rachel's. "No, we'd never do any such thing without your permission. Our only mission today is to encourage you to give him the same forgiveness you gave that boss person."

Rachel silently glowered Sue for some time. "What you guys don't seem to realize is that my boss beat me up, but my father ruined my whole life."

"Oh, Rachel," Suzanna let out a breath. "That's the tragedy of so many girls here. No one can change the past, but we can better understand it."

Pastor Sue searched her face with compassion. "No one is going to force you to see your father, but if you forgive him before God right now, that awful hatred will stop eating away at you. Then, if you could just face him *one* time, you'll feel a blessed relief inside. Remember how you felt better when you stopped hating that enforcer person?"

Rachel stood up as though she were about to leave, but she turned back to them. "Look, if I do this prayer and forgiveness thing, will you stop bugging me?"

The women stood up abruptly and each took one of her hands. Rachel's forgiveness prayer was offered hesitantly, but sincerely between her sobs.

FATHER

(God is) a father to the fatherless. He sets the
Lonely in families. PS 68: 5, 6

Rachel walked out of the school with halting steps toward Suzanna who stood beside her car, waving. She slipped off her new backpack and gave her a pained smile.

"Hop in. So, how was your first week back in the classroom?"

"No problem. I wish the boys wouldn't look at me though." She opened the car door, dropped the pack in and plopped into the seat. "Your teachers had me caught up to where this grade is—except for math, but I never was any good at math."

"We can work on that. Thanks for being right on time." She pulled out onto the street. "The place where you'll meet your Dad is just ten minutes from here."

"Look, about that: I know I said I would, but I'm thinking I could just write him a letter. Why do I have to forgive him in person?"

"Ah, Rachel," She gave her a sympathetic look. "You know we talked a lot about this encounter. A letter's just not the same. Remember, you don't have to like him, just forgive him and then say a few words about what you're doing and leave."

"This feels really awkward."

"I understand; I do, but you've rehearsed your lines, right? Let's hear it."

Rachel closed her eyes, raised her head and let out a big breath. "Hello, father—I wanted to say Mister Clemmons but pastor nixed that. Hello, father, I want you to know that I'm not happy with what you did, but I forgive you and won't hold it against you. I'm fine with my new life and won't need your help."

"That's it?"

"Why? How's that sound? "She waved a small piece of paper. "I've got it written down."

"Sounds pretty cold fish."

"Well, I'll tell him my address and say he can write. I just don't want any visits."

"Not even..." Suzanna pulled into a parking lot. "Not even an offer to come by for Thanksgiving or Christmas?"

"I'd rather not. Don't you realize how hard it's been for me to come this far?" She looked at Suzanna's pained expression. "Okay, if he asks, maybe Christmas."

Now parked, Suzanna got out and came around to Rachel's side and opened the door. "This is the church meeting hall. You don't have to stay long and I'll be right outside."

"When I come out, it's straight to the car and gone, okay?"

She took Rachel's hand as they went up the wooden steps. "I'm so proud of you, Rachel."

A lanky six-foot-six man in jeans and a new plaid shirt sat, shifting his weight on a folding chair beside a woman at the very front of the hall on a slightly raised stage.

His wife wore a light blue print dress, straight blond hair pushed back in a headband and an anxious smile. She massaged her husband's shoulder but stopped when the door at the far end of the hall opened.

Rachel began a determined brisk walk down the aisle between tables. Her father promptly got up, jumped off the stage and stopped to face her approach at the entrance to the aisle.

Her walk slowed and she halted ten feet from him. Rachel looked down at the paper in her hand. "Father—I..." She coughed. "Father, I want you to know..." She glanced up at her father who stood in silent patience.

Rachel coughed again, fumbled with her paper and mumbled to herself, "Oh, s__t."

She began again. "I'm not happy with what you did, but I forgive…"

Ronald Clemmons spoke softly. "It's okay Rachel. Take your time."

"You never wrote," she croaked.

"Oh, sweetheart, I sent you dozens of letters from prison."

Her face furrowed in puzzlement before she realized. "Mother!"

Rachel dropped her arms and stood looking at her father. His expression of deep love and compassion flowed into her soul and tears began to stream down Rachel's cheeks. The paper fell to the floor. She sprinted to her father, jumped up and threw her arms around him. With her cheek pressed against his chest she sobbed, "Daddy, oh *Daddy*, why did you have to leave?"

His tears dripped on her face and mingled with hers as he held her close. "Never again, precious Rey-rey. Never *ever* again."

She looked up into his face. "You didn't have to steal. We could have gotten by."

"I know, Darlin'. Rey-rey, I'm so sorry. It was a horrible mistake. I was just trying to get money for us, but I didn't know how to pray or trust God then."

Rachel embraced her father again, this time in silence. She felt a soft warm hand on the side of her neck, and glanced up to see the smiling woman who joined them. The woman said,

"Hi, I'm Liz, your Dad's wife. Ron has missed you something awful. We're so glad we finally found you."

Ron put one arm around Rachel and one around Liz. "Rachel, I prayed that you would find it in your heart to forgive me. Do you think you ever can?"

A grin had spread over Rachel's face and she chuckled, "Forgive you?" She pulled back to look him in the eye. "Oh *yes*, Daddy. I guess I completely forgot to say—but only if you *promise* never to leave again."

Suzanna cracked the door open to peek in. She stood with her knuckle in her teeth and radiant delight in her eyes. She quietly murmured, "Oh, praise you dear Lord. This is *so* of you."

As the family embraced again, Liz kissed Rachel on the head. "He *better* not leave. We're going to be a family of four before Christmas."

ACKNOWLEDGEMENTS

I deeply appreciate all those who helped make this book take shape. In my church I am profoundly touched as I observe real Christian families in action. Parents and children living under God's love takes my breath away. While the story is fictitious, seven year old Kali is a real child evangelist and she appears on the back cover. Kali said she would like to audition for the movie version. (We'll see.)

In my research, I met some dedicated people working in missions to rehabilitate victims of human trafficking. Together Freedom operates a rehabilitation facility that inspired my fictitious "Saveher Ranch." Eileen Fernandez from that organization proof read an early draft and offered welcome suggestions and corrections. In a presentation by Jaime Johnson, representing Sisters of the Streets, I learned about the difficulty in approaching trafficking victims directly, and that former victims would refer to themselves as "survivors" rather than rescued. Another organization is the Association for the Recovery of Children, or ARC. In a presentation of their work, Tina Paulson described a recovery method similar to the one I wrote about. Two Worlds Connect is a music ministry to raise awareness and help survivors. (Note their statement below.)

The interior drawings are the artistry of Wyatt "Dazed" Holcomb. The back cover painting is a portion of a larger work by Doreen Terryberry. My heartfelt thanks to all.

Pascal John Imperato began writing Fiction in Junior High, became a High School literary editor, and continued short stories in Creative Writing classes at Johns Hopkins University. Getting a Medical Degree at Duke University, and beginning a medical practice in Pennsylvania temporarily resulted in scientific and journal writing. After a born again revelation, he resumed fiction writing once more, but with a messianic twist under the pen name of "John Pascal." He has published Sci-Fi: "The Revelation Trilogy" novels: "The Bee," "Domes," and "2248." Also a two book angel series: "Wingin' It," and "My Child." "PRISONER 1171" is a novel focusing on the disabled and evangelism in prison.

Pascal lives and writes in Fallbrook California.

AUTHOR'S NOTE

When one opens ones heart to do a work for the Lord, one is often surprised to find Him working beside you. I am completely humbled by His presence, often revealed by "God winks." When He asked me to write about human trafficking, I argued with Him. (Ha, ha.) The next week our church had a symposium on the subject. God's message for me: "Get to work, son."

THE REAL GOOD GUYS

TOGETHER FREEDOM SAN DIEGO is a volunteer action team that includes case managers and mentors who have been trained, certified, and background checked by FACESS' Together Freedom (TogetherFreedom.org) to provide services to trafficking victims in San Diego county and surrounding areas. Our volunteer team provides and collaborates with other service providers to provide immediate wrap-around care, shelter and rehabilitation for American girls (minors or adults) who are victims of sex trafficking and sexual slavery in the U.S. Our collaborative program coordinates law enforcement, government agencies, public service agencies, non-government organizations, professionals, churches and volunteer groups to successfully intervene and provide victim advocacy in the rescue of victims of sex trafficking. We offer trauma-informed, compassionate care, support and provision for their immediate needs as well as coordinate with professionals to offer them immediate medical, legal and psychological assistance.
Eileen Fernandez. Information at "togetherfreedom.org"

Two Worlds Connect Productions, Inc is a 501(c)(3) whose prime directive is to make a difference in the world by identifying problems, needs, promoting awareness, education, and helping with solutions. We chose the universal language of music as our platform. Close to our hearts is putting an end to all forms of slavery, including human trafficking at home and abroad. Concerts and outings are provided for survivors of human trafficking as these women rebuild their lives.
Sue & Ed Williams. Information at "Twoworldsconnect.com"

52705928R00124

Made in the USA
San Bernardino, CA
27 August 2017